GIVE UP THE GHOST

THE GHOST DETECTIVE SERIES #2

JANE HINCHEY

For my insider team, Fleur, Misty, Dana, Lilly, Lisa, and Marcia you guys are the BEST!

Never in my almost thirty years did I think my new normal would be talking to ghosts, yet here we are.

After inheriting a PI business, I find my clients are more incorporeal than not and are relying on me to solve their untimely deaths. Unfortunately, being a magnet for ghosts has its downside. Hello? Lack of privacy, for starters. Not to mention looking like a looney tune for holding animated conversations with myself. But the biggest problem? Their killers don't want me on the case.

Now I have a new mystery to solve. Local psychic Myra Hansen woke up dead and she's none too happy about it. *Seems she didn't see that one coming!* Together with my ghostly best friend, a talking cat, and Captain Cowboy Hot Pants—or, as he likes to be called, Detective Kade Galloway—I'm in yet another race against time.

Catch a killer before the killer catches me.

Join Audrey Fitzgerald in the Ghost Detective series, a

paranormal cozy mystery featuring a talking cat, a ghost, and a murder to solve.

AUTHOR'S NOTE

Hey! Welcome to the weird and wacky world of my imagination. I hope you enjoy your time here.

If you love anything supernatural as much as I do, then you're going to enjoy the journey ahead - at least I think you will.

Give up the Ghost is the second book in my Ghost Detective series, with more to come, so make sure you sign up for my newsletter to get notifications on when the next book is ready.

You can sign up for my newsletter here:
Janehinchey.com/join-my-newsletter

Okay, ready to weave some magic and solve some mysteries?

I'll see you on the other side!

xoxo

Jane

*T*here was a dead man sitting in my living room. Since it was way too early for anything resembling civilized conversation, I ignored him and padded the five steps to my kitchen, yawning and scratching my butt. My apartment was on the small side, a boho broom closet would have been a more apt description so the journey from bed to coffee nirvana was a small one. My name is Audrey Fitzgerald. Fitz to some. And recently I've gained the ability to see and talk to ghosts. And a cat. Other than that I'm perfectly normal, I swear.

Moving on auto pilot I opened the overhead cupboard, blindly felt around for a pod, shoved it into my Keurig and hit the magical button, then raided my fridge for anything remotely edible. Pickings were slim. There were some suspect green and fuzzy items at the back, then I spotted a leftover slice of meat lover's pizza—how had I missed that? With a little yip of joy, I tossed it in the microwave. Today was going to be a good day, I could feel it in my bones. Any day that started with leftover pizza was a winner in my book. The microwave beeped, and I immediately shoved the pizza slice into my mouth, ignoring the searing temperature and the very real possibility I'd just removed one hundred layers of flesh from the roof of my mouth. It was worth it.

Through watering eyes I fixed my coffee, carried the rest of the pizza slice over to the sofa and sank into it, looking at the dead man who was waiting patiently for me to acknowledge him.

"You know, I'm not really fond of mornings." I said.

"Pizza too hot?" he drawled. If he was trying not to smile, he failed.

"Not at all." I lied, poking the roof of my mouth with my tongue, schooling my features to not give away the horror at discovering the flap of loose skin I'd scorched off.

His smirk gave way to a full-blown laugh. "Give

it up Fitz, if your glassy eyes weren't proof enough, the way you're sucking your cheeks in and out is a dead giveaway."

I glared at him, refusing to admit he was right. My stubborn streak kicked in and with my eyes locked on his I defiantly stuffed the rest of the pizza into my mouth, worked my jaw to chew and sent a stern message to my eyeballs to stop watering.

"You know if you choke, I can't save you?" he said conversationally. I held up one finger, signaling him to hold that thought, while I chewed. And chewed. And chewed. After swallowing, I took a sip of coffee which only intensified the scalding in my mouth— nothing builds character like nerves of steel—then calmly lowered the mug, resting it on one thigh, ignoring the heat searing through my pj's. A coffee ring burn would look cool, right?

"What can I do for you this fine morning, Ben?" Ben Delaney was my best friend. And he'd died. Correction, he'd been murdered and now instead of live Ben, I had ghost Ben. And his cat, Thor, who was not a ghost, but for some unholy reason I could now understand and speak to. I told you, totally normal.

"Why don't you move into my house?" Ben shook his head, his eyes traveling around my shoebox of a home, "It would be so much easier for you. The office is there. Thor is there. He misses you, you know."

"Pft, he's a furry little jerk who doesn't give a damn as long as his food bowl is full." Ben's cat aside, he had a point. Ben had left me everything in his will. And I mean everything. His house. His car. His PI business. Audrey Fitzgerald, temp extraordinaire, was now Audrey Fitz, PI in training. And I worked out of Ben's home office.

But for some reason I couldn't bring myself to move into Ben's house. His car, on the other hand? Who could turn down a metallic gray Nissan Rogue SUV with charcoal leather seats? Not this girl, certainly not when my set of wheels was a 1970 blue Chrysler. As it was, I commuted backwards and forwards between Ben's house and mine and it worked fine. As long as I pushed down the guilt that I left Thor to his own devices for such lengthy periods. Despite my protests to the contrary, I was secretly fond of the big gray cat that resembled a teddy bear.

"Did you want something?" I deflected. We'd been over this ad nauseam and if I knew what was holding me back from moving, I'd have done something about it because yes, Ben's house was ten times better than my apartment. I knew it. He knew it. Thor definitely knew it. But each time the subject came up, I baulked, like a filly at its first hurdle, so much so I refused to discuss it anymore.

"How's the case going?" He asked. I acknowledged his change of subject with a nod. Smart ghost. "It's done." I beamed, proud of myself. As a PI in training, I had to clock fifteen hundred hours with supervision before I could sit my exam and get my official private investigator license. Lucky for me, Captain Cowboy Hot Pants, or as he likes to be called Detective Kade Galloway, agreed to be my supervisor. He pretty much lets me do my own thing and signs off on my weekly reports. Since Ben's death I'd not only solved his murder, I'd recovered a missing prized chihuahua, and solved the great gnome mystery of Firefly Bay. Someone had been stealing gnomes from gardens and leaving them on rooftops along the main strip. Turns out it wasn't someone, it was several someones and was a practical joke started by some high school kids. Still, I broke the case, and that's what counts.

I regaled Ben with an extra lengthy description of the great gnome mystery of Firefly Bay, watched as his eyes became glassy, could pinpoint the exact moment when he stopped listening. It wasn't difficult, he literally disappeared. It was a quirk I'd noticed recently. Whenever Ben was disinterested, he'd slowly become more and more incorporeal until poof, he wasn't there anymore. I'd quizzed him on where ghosts went when they weren't haunting someone and he'd taken great exception to the term haunting and we'd spent over an hour debating the term and I'd never gotten an answer. From what I knew he didn't sleep, he wasn't restricted in where he went—which came in handy during investigations, Ben could slip inside and scout around undetected, whereas I, on the other hand, could get arrested for breaking and entering.

Therefore, when my phone rang, and I wasted precious minutes searching for it—I eventually located it under my bed—he wasn't around to hear the details of my next case. As much as I loved Ben, and I did dearly, he could be a little... smothering. Just because he used to be a police officer and then a private investigator didn't mean he got to tell me what to do. And yes, I know, he calls it guidance and training since it is technically his PI business I've taken over, but sometimes a girl needs a little elbow room, a little space to get things done herself.

I pushed down the little twang of pique that emerged when I applied the same principles to

Captain Cowboy Hot Pants. Because, contrary to what I wanted from Ben, I did not want from Kade Galloway. A little attention would be... nice. But after the rather unfortunate incident when I'd been dosed with Crimson Bark, which FYI has the unpleasant side effect of explosive diarrhea, and said Detective had witnessed said aftermath—much to my utter mortification. Lets not even mention the fact that I'd been dressed in nothing but panties and a T-shirt at the time, I'd been expecting... something. Flowers? Chocolates? A date? Color me surprised when none of that happened. And color me even more surprised that I'm sitting here wishing it had. Me? Date a cop? Madness.

Shaking myself out of that particular daydream, I got dressed, snatched up my bag, tripped over the rug I've tripped over a million times before but refuse to move, and headed out the door to meet my new client.

2

"Down on the ground! Hands on your heads!"

I dropped to the floor along with five other customers in Firefly Bay Community Bank, not believing my misfortune. I'd only stopped in to sign a document that had been missed when I'd been added to Delaney Investigations bank account. The red tape had been phenomenal, they'd actually wanted to talk to Ben, which I'd pointed out wasn't possible due to him not being alive anymore. Instead, I'd produced his death certificate and his will. Again. Dealing with the bank was up there with one of the most painful experiences of my life. I'd rather have my hoo-ha waxed, and that's saying something!

Face thrust into the carpet, I tried not to think of how many dirty shoes had walked across it, treading God only knows what into the fibers. Fibers that my face was now intimately pressed against. Instead, I snuck a peek out the corner of my eye. Three men. All on the taller side. Slim builds. Denim jeans, black hoodies, clown masks covering their faces. I screwed my eyes tightly closed for a second, sucking in a steadying breath. Why did they have to choose clowns? Clowns got such a bad rap, they really weren't the evil creatures some people made them out to be. Yet seeing a clown waving around a big ass gun and threatening to blow your head off if you so much as twitched was doing absolutely nothing for their reputation.

The Firefly Bay Community Bank had undergone renovations a while back, ditching a regular counter that segregated the staff from the customers and instead going for that whole open plan thing, with desks at different stations, machines in one wall taking care of all your cash needs. The opposite wall housed floor to ceiling monitors that displayed one giant video loop. I bet the staff were regretting this new layout now, exposed as they were out here with us. No big counter with a hidden alarm. No security screen to activate, keeping the robbers away. Instead, the tellers were on the floor with the rest of us.

"Get your asses over here!" One of the robbers growled. Only with our faces buried in the floor, we had no idea who he was referring too. His robber mates, or us? And where, exactly, did we need to be? My questions were answered when I felt the press of a metal barrel between my shoulder blades. "On your hands and knees and crawl over there with the others." I did as instructed, crawling to join a handful of customers several feet away in the middle of the room. *Jennifer—or was it Judith? Jessica?* Anyway, the staff member who I'd dropped in to meet with and sign that one final ever so important document, crawled alongside me, her face pale, her lips trembling.

Once we reached the main group, we eased down onto our stomachs to lay flat on the floor once more. But the brief journey had given me a chance to look around. The man who'd pressed his gun into my back stood between us and the front doors, which were now locked, I'd seen him reach up and deactivate the automatic sliding mechanism. I thought I'd glimpsed a tattoo on the inside of his wrist, but I was too far away to make it out.

One of the other robbers had a backpack and was

going around collecting cell phones, wallets and purses, dumping them into the bag. When it was my turn I wriggled, easing the phone out of my back pocket. It slipped and fell to the floor. Not a big fall considering my current position. I reached for it, fingers fumbling, flinching when the robber shouted at me, "Hurry up!" I finally got a grip on the phone and dropped it into the backpack, mourning the loss. It was new. I'd only had it a little while, had finally replaced my old, broken up and only just hanging in there model. And now my shiny new phone was gone.

I watched the man with the backpack move away, taking my phone with him, before dragging my eyes away to search for the third robber. He was at a door leading to the rear of the bank. I assumed that's where the safe was. After all, all the automatic teller machines had to be kept stocked, deposits had to be taken care of. Despite the human race moving toward a cashless society, there was still plenty of cash around and these guys knew it.

He and the man with the backpack had a brief, hushed discussion. Backpack man turned to where we were all huddled on the floor, eyes searching before coming to rest on a man laying opposite me.

"You!" Backpack man growled. "Up!" He prodded

the man's leg with his gun to give him extra incentive to get a move on. The man scrambled to his feet, eyes terrified. He was young, early twenties, dressed in gray trousers and a blue polo shirt with the bank's logo on it. Backpack man prodded him in the back with his gun, steering him toward the closed door. The other robber moved aside, and the penny dropped. On the wall next to the door was a keypad. They needed a code to get through.

"Unlock it." Backpack man snarled. I lifted my head a little higher to watch. The employee punched in his code. There was a beep, and the door clicked open. Backpack man kept his gun trained on the employee and pushed him through the door ahead of him.

A nudge from the barrel of a gun pressed against the back of my neck had me flattening myself to the floor. "Stay down!"

I'd kinda forgotten about the gun wielding robber behind us and gotten a little too enthusiastic with watching what was happening. Jennifer, Judith or Jessica reached out to me, touching my arm. "Are you okay?" She whispered. I gave a small nod and was about to open my mouth to answer when a booted foot appeared in my line of vision. "If you two don't shut up, I will put a bullet in her brain.

Understood?" I knew whose brain he was talking about because I could feel the barrel of the gun pressing against my skull. Jennifer-Judith-Jessica made a little yip noise and screwed her eyes shut.

Thankfully, his attention was diverted away from me when the door the other two had disappeared through slammed open and they came barreling through, shouting, "Alarm's been tripped. Time to go."

"Shit. Did you get anything?" The floor vibrated by my head as a booted foot stepped over me.

"Yeah, but not what we came for." I chanced another look. Backpack man was now carrying an extra sports bag, black, nondescript. The other man had a matching one. How much money would two sports bags hold?

"On your feet, bitch." It was my turn to yip in surprise when I was grabbed by the arm and dragged to my feet. "You're so keen to watch then you can stick your head out the front door and check for cops."

Oh, goody. Lucky me. With my upper arm in a death grip, I had no choice but to go along as he dragged me toward the glass sliding doors. Reaching up with his free hand, he unlocked the doors, and they slid open.

"Don't try anything stupid," the gunman said.

"Okay." I wasn't entirely sure what he wanted me to do, so I slowly stepped onto the sidewalk. I glanced left, then right.

"What do you see?" the gunman asked. I looked back at him over my shoulder, saw the barrel of his gun trained on me. "No cops?" I squeaked.

"You sure? You don't sound sure, and if it turns out you're lying, you're gonna get a bullet."

I double checked up and down the street. "No cops." I said again, with a ton more conviction. A bullet was not in my plans for today. Although neither was being smack damn in the middle of a bank heist either.

I stood there, motionless in the middle of the sidewalk, feeling awkward and exposed. What if the cops arrived and thought I was a robber? What if the robbers decided to leave no witnesses and shoot me after all? I wasn't a huge fan of either of those scenarios. The sound of screeching tires caught my attention, and I swiveled, lost my balance and staggered across the sidewalk while spotting a white van tearing down the road. It pulled up at the curb.

"Lets go!" The three bandits bolted out of the bank, pushing past and totally ignoring me as they climbed into the van and it tore off with another screech of rubber. I reached for my phone to snap the number plate. Belatedly remembering I no longer had my phone, they'd taken it with them. Instead, I tried to memorize the plates, only they were already too far away to read. In the distance I heard the wail of sirens and sure enough a cop car came hurtling around the same corner the white van had mere moments earlier. I pointed. "That way! They went that way. White van. Three men, armed." I shouted. The officer in the passenger seat rolled down the window "Thanks ma'am, another patrol unit is on its way. Stay put." And they were gone, tearing off after the white van.

I made my way back into the bank where the hostages were getting to their feet. Everyone rattled and talking at once. Jennifer-Judith-Jessica came rushing up to me. "Oh my goodness, Audrey, are you okay?" She slung an arm around my shoulders and led me to her workstation, practically shoving me into a chair whether or not I wanted to sit. Another police car arrived, its strobe lights reflecting in a kaleidoscope of red and blue across the interior of the bank. Officer Walsh and Sergeant Powell appeared in the doorway, guns drawn. A dozen people all sucking in their breath at the same time was the only sound. We froze, not wanting to make any sudden moves and accidentally find ourselves shot.

They swept the room then holstered their weapons before radioing in their findings and then began interviewing witnesses. Jennifer-Judith-Jessica fussed around me while I sat silently and watched Sergeant Powell interview the male staff member who'd punched in the code that let the robbers into the rear of the bank. I strained to listen, thought I heard him say he'd added an extra hash key, which was a trigger to indicate the door was being unlocked under duress.

Out of the corner of my eye I spotted a pair of black denim-clad legs stroll through the front door and my heart did a little skip in my chest. Detective Galloway made his way to the employee who'd punched in the code that simultaneously opened the door but also triggered the alarm. As he listened to the man's story his eyes swept the bank, brushed over me, then did a classic double take. "Hold that thought." He said to the young man.

"Audrey Fitzgerald." I wasn't sure if that was a greeting, or a question.

"Yes?"

His gray eyes burned into me, taking in every detail, from my worn jeans, to my Abba T-shirt, to the fact that I was being pressed into my seat by Jennifer-Judith-Jessica's firm hand on my shoulder. I don't know why she felt I needed to sit, but each time I'd tried to shrug off her hand she'd merely gripped harder. I figured it was easier to give in. "You're hurt?"

Again, I wasn't sure if it was a question or a statement, so I merely shrugged. "You know me, always getting into scrapes."

"I'll call an ambulance." He was already reaching for his phone. My hand shot out, fingers wrapping around his wrist, a brief jolt of electricity shooting up my arm at the contact. "No! Please, I don't need an ambulance. I'm fine. I'm not hurt at all, I think Jennifer-Judith-Jessica here is in shock and has deemed it necessary to keep me pinned to this chair. Seriously, I do not want or need another trip to hospital, I'm one visit away from winning a set of steak knives and a free trip to Bermuda."

His lips twitched. "And that would be a bad thing?"

"Hello? Have you even heard of the Bermuda triangle? And seriously? Me? With steak knives? Now that's just asking for trouble." I had what my family liked to call the clumsy gene. I'm usually sporting a bruise from some minor altercation with an inanimate object, and if there's a beverage to be knocked over, you could guarantee I'd be the one to do it.

Galloway held up a finger in front of my face. "How many fingers am I holding up?"

"One." I promptly replied. Now was not the time to mention that a headache was starting to pound behind my eyes, as a result, I'm sure, of the sudden adrenaline rush that was now receding. As soon as I showed the slightest sign of weakness, I knew what would happen. He'd have me in a patrol car and up to the hospital before I could say Captain Cowboy Hot Pants. Plus, I needed to remember that I was mad at him. Just when I was softening my stance about cops, he goes and does this. And by this I mean he doesn't ask me out on a date.

3

"*J*eez, Fitz. I can't leave you alone for one second without you getting into trouble." Ben materialized by my side and I shot clean out of my chair, a garbled yelp that had everyone in the bank turning to look my way. I cleared my throat. "Sorry. I'm fine, really, go back to what you were doing." I told them, tugging at the hem of my T-shirt self-consciously.

Galloway gave me a searing look, and I blinked. "What?" I said defensively, feeling a wave of heat travel up my neck and into my cheeks.

"Is there anything you want to tell me?" He asked, crossing his arms.

The corners of my mouth turned down, and I shook my head. "Nope, don't think so." I absolutely did not want to tell him I could talk to ghosts. He'd have me locked in the looney bin faster than I could blink.

"You're sure?" He pressed.

I nodded. "Positive." Then added, "any idea how long this will take? Only I have a new client that I'm meant to be meeting..." Anything to distract him from the fact that I was twitching and jumping like a raccoon on crack.

"A new client?" Galloway and Ben spoke simultaneously. I ignored Ben in favor of Galloway. "Yes. Jill Murray. Missing goldfish."

Ben snorted, and I jerked my head to shoot him a glare. Okay. So it wasn't a big case, in fact it probably wasn't much of a case at all, I mean it's highly unlikely the goldfish had gotten out of his bowl and gone for a walk, but still, Jill had phoned me in a panic and it was my duty, as a PI, to investigate. And I took my duty seriously. Although admittedly I was itching to investigate the bank robbery I was unwittingly a part of.

"Right." Galloway nodded, then glanced at his watch. "This will take a while, I'm afraid."

"Oh." This would not look good, me standing up a prospective new client. I chewed my lip, thinking. I couldn't call her, the thieves had taken my phone.

Just as I had the thought Galloway shoved his phone under my nose. "Here. Use this and call them. Reschedule."

I took the phone from him, felt the spark of heat where our fingers brushed, felt the color in my cheeks intensify and ignored Ben who was back to teasing me about my reaction. "Why don't you just kiss him already?" Ben asked, nudging me with his elbow, which resulted in an icy blast to my ribs and internal organs.

"Quit it." I whispered, wriggling to dispel the icy sensation.

"You say something?" Galloway asked.

"I said, thank you. Ummm. You go ahead, I'll bring this back to you once I'm done." I really needed him to walk away so I could talk to Ben, and not about a missing goldfish. Galloway cocked his head, seemed to have some sort of internal dialogue himself, then gave a brief nod and swiveled on his heel, returning to the young employee who'd punched in the code.

"You better make it quick." Ben said, "he's going to need his phone back."

"Right." I googled Jill Murray, found her phone number and called her, explaining that I wouldn't be able to keep our appointment today.

"I left you a message, dear." She told me, voice dripping in sadness. "Mr. Murray just called me to say that Kevin had died, and he'd flushed him down the toilet before he left for work. He didn't want me to get up and see Kevin floating belly up, so he took care of it, only the silly man didn't think to tell me."

"Oh, well, that's great. I mean, not great that Kevin is dead that's awful and I'm sorry for your loss. But at least now you know..." I trailed off.

"Thank you, dear." Jill sniffed and then hung up. I kept the phone to my ear and turned to look at Ben. "Where were you? I could have used you here today."

"Yeah sorry, your rendition of the great gnome catastrophe was my undoing. I went to check on dad."

"It wasn't a catastrophe." I grumbled. "It was a mystery. But never mind that now. How about you go see what's on the other side of that door? I assume a safe? Is there anything else back there? Safety deposit boxes? I want to know what the thieves were after because once they realized the alarm had been triggered they said they didn't get what they came for. And how did they know the alarm had been triggered?"

Ben stood and stretched. "Okay, okay, I'll go take

a look. As for the alarm, they'd probably be a light, alerting the back office staff."

"Back office staff?"

"Yeah, the staff who aren't out here. The Manager, for one. There's work that has to happen in a bank that isn't customer facing." He glanced around. "And I'm not seeing workstations out here, just service desks, so I'd say there's probably an office pod back there."

"Right. Well, go look. Please. I've got to give this phone back—" I gasped, a thought suddenly striking me. "My phone! We can track it. I have the *find my phone* app installed." Ben grinned at me giving me a knowing look like he'd already thought of that but was letting me have this little victory.

"I'd imagine almost everyone whose phone was taken has some sort of tracking app. It was a rookie move on their behalf, taking your phones." He said, then crossed the room and walked straight through the security door. Shaking my head, I stood and carried Galloway's phone back to him. "Thank you. Crisis averted; Kevin the goldfish has been found." I said.

"A water burial?" Galloway asked. I nodded. "Sadly, yes. He'd died and Jill's husband disposed of his body before leaving for work but didn't think to tell his wife. But, I had a thought, the robbers took our phones—we can track them." I finished in a rush, excited with my idea.

"No need. We have recovered the phones." Galloway said, grinning at my shocked expression. "Patrol got reports of a white van dumping something in a bin down near the wharf. They recovered six mobile phones. They're on the way back here now so the phones can be identified and returned to their owners."

My shoulders slumped. I'd had the crazy notion that we'd be able to track the phones right into the thieves' den. Sadly, it was not that easy. But I perked up at the thought that I'd have my phone back. "And the van?" I asked.

"No sign of it. Probably parked up in a garage or warehouse."

"It's my fault." I muttered, scuffing my foot on the carpet. If only I'd gotten the number plate. But it had all happened so fast and I'd been convinced they would shoot me. I hadn't been thinking clearly, and that worried me, because a PI needed to be thinking clearly at all times.

"What is?" Galloway paused doing whatever he was doing with his phone, one dark brow arched.

"I didn't get their number plate. I was right

there." I pointed out the front windows. "I was in the perfect position to get their number and I didn't."

He crossed his arms. "Did you try?"

"Well... yeah. I reached for my phone, thinking I'd snap a photo and get the plates from that. Only I didn't have my phone and by the time I realized that they were too far away for me to make out the plate."

"Then that's all that matters." He said, "that it occurred to you to do that."

"That's not useful." I grumbled, still annoyed at myself. I didn't want platitudes or words to make me feel better. I dropped the ball, and that's all there was to it.

Galloway sighed, "I wasn't going to tell you this because I really don't want you investigating this one, yet somehow I get the feeling you're not going to be able to help yourself."

My head snapped up. "Tell me what?"

"The plates had been removed from the van. So even if you had managed to snap a photo, it wouldn't have made a difference."

"How do you know that? About the plates being removed, I mean."

"The patrol car got close enough to see." He rested a hand on my shoulder. "But I mean it Audrey, you need to stay out of this one."

I bristled. *What? He didn't think I was smart enough?* "Why?" I demanded, ready to be outraged.

"These guys are armed and violent. Consider yourself lucky you didn't get shot. You have had no arms training, don't have your gun license. This one is dangerous and best left to the police."

"Oh." He had a point. I'd never shot a gun in my life. Despite Ben offering to teach me on several occasions I'd always shied away from them, figuring a person as clumsy as me should never be in charge of a firearm.

There was a commotion at the door and I turned to see Officer Collier walk in, plastic bag in hand, carrying our phones. Galloway dropped his hand from my shoulder and said, "wait here," before joining him. I turned my attention to the young man who'd sounded the alarm.

"How are you holding up?" I asked him. He slid his hands into his pockets and studied his feet, mumbling "Okay, I guess."

"It was pretty scary." I continued. "I've never been involved in something like this before... have you? Do they train you for this? Because I thought you were very brave. And smart." I added, nodding toward the keypad on the wall.

He straightened a little at the praise, his blue eyes

carrying that dazed look where you can't really believe what's just happened.

"To be honest, I was shitting myself." He admitted, running a hand around the back of his neck. "I was cursing that they picked me, out of all the staff out front."

"All the staff? Isn't it just you and Jennifer-Judith-Jessica?" I asked, glancing around the bank, my eyes landing on the female staff member who I'd been here to see. I did a quick count in my head. Two staff and four customers, including myself, had been out front during the holdup.

"Who?" He frowned, then turned to where I was looking. "You mean Susan?" Then he shrugged. "Well yeah, she's senior to me. Man, I feel bad that I wished they'd chosen her instead of me... but it's the truth."

"What's your name? I'm Audrey Fitzgerald." I offered, holding out my hand. He shook it, his handshake weak, his fingers clammy. "Jacob Henry."

"At least you remembered the code thing, Jacob," I smiled, trying to put him at ease. "That saved us."

"I'm just glad it worked." Jacob was pale under his lightly tanned skin, his short brown hair standing up randomly where he'd run his fingers through it. I figured he was in shock and patted him on the back in what I hoped was a soothing gesture.

"Any idea what they were after?"

He snorted. "Money!" The way he said it, as if I were a simpleton, had me bristling, but then maybe he hadn't overheard what I had, that the robbers themselves didn't get what they came for.

"But you have safety deposit boxes here, right?" I pressed. "Did they try to access any of them?"

He looked down at me, blue eyes puzzled. "No, straight to the vault."

"And the vault was open?"

"It was. It has a two-minute delay, but we were expecting a cash delivery so the manager opened it early so as not to waste time." My eyebrows shot up. I bet that was a big breach of protocol. Kinda negated the entire purpose of having a time delay lock. I made a mental note to talk to Ben about it.

"What time is the delivery due?"

"It was meant to be here at nine but they called to say they'd been delayed in traffic. A six car pile-up out on the highway, so they were running late." So the robbers had known cash was being delivered to the bank today and what time it was expected. What they didn't know was that it had been delayed.

"Who else knew about this? That the bank was getting a cash delivery today?"

Jacob shrugged. "It's not exactly a secret, but we don't advertise the fact either. All the bank staff knew. Some customers too. We don't need to order cash in that frequently, maybe twice a year if that." Before he could say anything more Officer Collier approached with the plastic bag.

"Audrey. Jacob. I need you to identify your phone's please."

"We get them back, right?" I asked, "You're not keeping them for evidence or anything?"

"You get them back. We've logged them. I will get you to check your call logs to double check the suspects haven't used them to make a call or send a message—in which case, we will hold the phone."

I searched through my phone, showed Officer Collier my call log. The phone hadn't been used since this morning when Jill Murray had called about her missing goldfish. There was one missed call from the same number—her ringing back to say the mystery had been solved I assumed. He nodded, made a note of it and turned his attention to Jacob. Jacob's phone was in a Star Wars case and I leaned over to get a closer look. He had a lot of outgoing calls to the same number. And I mean a lot. At least twenty this morning alone.

"Whose number is that?" Officer Collier asked, examining the call log with interest. "Did you make all these calls?"

"It's my wife. Emily." Jacob said defensively. I blinked in surprise. Jacob looked way too young to be married.

Officer Collier stared at him. "You always call your wife this much?"

"She didn't pick up." Jacob muttered, looking at his shoes. Officer Collier and I shared a knowing look. She didn't pick up because she didn't want to talk to him—obviously—only why keep calling? Why not leave a voicemail and get on with your day? Ah, the perils of young love.

"What's so urgent that you needed to call her this many times?" Officer Collier asked, suspicion dripping from his voice. My mouth dropped open. Was this an inside job? Had Jacob been working with the robbers? But that didn't make sense. He'd tripped the alarm. And he truly looked awful, pale skin and clammy hands. But maybe that wasn't from shock? Maybe it was fear, fear he was about to get caught for doing something very, very, bad. There had been a fourth person involved in the holdup. The getaway driver. And it could easily have been a woman, I hadn't gotten a look at them at all. Maybe Jacob was in on the whole thing and his wife too.

"Did she know about today's cash delivery?" I asked, interrupting Officer Collier, who gave me an annoyed glance.

Jacob bristled. "She did not. We're separated. I haven't talked to her in over a month."

"Not for lack of trying." Officer Collier replied drolly, signing off on Jacob's phone and moving on to the next person, apparently satisfied with Jacob's answer.

4

"*I* can't believe you just did that!" Over the ringing in my ears, I could hear Ben's high-pitched screeching.

"Calm down. It'll buff out." I assured him.

"Buff out? Buff out!" His screech kicked up a couple more octaves. "Audrey, you totaled my car. In case you didn't notice, it's on its roof and you're dangling upside down."

"You know, now that you mention it," I grumbled, pushing my hair out of my face, "I did notice that myself. But thanks for pointing it out."

I watched as Ben paced back and forth in front of me. Okay for him, he was incorporeal. A ghost. When the car had flipped rather spectacularly and skidded along the road in a shower of sparks and cuss words, he'd been fine. He was already dead, he couldn't die again. I, on the other hand, could. I assessed my current situation. I wasn't hurt—much. Couple of bruises, tops. But I was stuck, upside down, pinned in the driver's seat by the seat belt.

I tugged at it again and pressed the release catch. Nothing. The radio cut in and out, a combination of some talk back show and static. The bent metal of the car body creaked and groaned as it settled into its new shape. The soft tinkle as another tiny piece of shattered glass fell to the road. Later I knew I'd mourn the loss of my beautiful Nissan Rogue. Okay, Ben's Nissan Rogue, but since his untimely death and my subsequent inheritance, the car was now mine. And I'd just totaled it. But that wasn't the worst of my problems.

"Are they coming?" I asked, tugging at the belt feverishly and twisting to try to get a glimpse of the road behind us.

Ben stopped pacing and temporarily disappeared from view, before reappearing in front of me, making me squeak in surprise. "Geez. A little warning." We were mostly adjusted to our new normal. Ben as a ghost and all the quirks that came with it, but he still surprised me with his sudden appearances.

"Yes." He said. He was crouched in front of me, eyes running over me, lingering on the stuck catch of the seat belt. While his incorporeal status came in handy from time to time, now was not one of those occasions. He couldn't help me. Not physically.

My ears picked up the sound of an approaching vehicle, and a shiver ran up my spine. With my heartbeat thundering in my ears I continued to tug at the belt, then tried wriggling out of it, but the blood was rushing to my head and the belt would not let me go that easily. "Can you see my phone anywhere?" I asked. Ben began searching, moving in and out of the car's body, which should have been horrifying but I was too worried about getting my ass out of here before the bad guys arrived to worry about Ben and his ghostly apparition status.

Too late. The vehicle I'd heard approaching had arrived. Headlights swept around the bend, the engine settling into a gentle rumble as it rolled to a halt. The beams of light cut through the night air, blinding me. Raising an arm, I shielded my face while my free hand frantically pressed the seatbelt catch like I was sending out a Morse code message. Car doors slammed and multiple footsteps approached. This was it. I was doomed. I braced myself, waiting for the hail of bullets.

When none were forthcoming, I paused in my frantic button pressing efforts and peeked out from behind my arm. All I could see were legs. Two sets, dressed in dark pants and boots.

One of the legs crouched and shone a flashlight directly in my face. "You okay in there?" The voice sounded suspiciously like Firefly Bays one and only Officer Ian Mills. Of all the damn luck.

"All good thanks." I flashed my teeth in a grimace smile combo. "Could you not point that in my face? Please." For once Mills did as requested and moved the beam of light out of my retinas, instead flashing it around the interior of my mangled car. "Single vehicle roll-over." He said to the companion over his shoulder.

"I'll call it in." I peered beyond Mills, surprised to see Officer Sarah Jacobs. Mills usually partnered with Sergeant Dwight Clements—both of them incompetent buffoons, so color me surprised to see Officer Jacobs in attendance. I listened as she spoke into the mic attached to her shoulder. "Single vehicle roll-over. Female driver requiring extraction. Request fire and ambulance."

"You drunk?" Mills had finished his rudimentary exam of my car and shone his flashlight directly in my eyes again. Blinded, I reared back, raising my hands to cover my eyes. "Jesus Christ!" I cursed, "Quit with the light would you. I might need my eyeballs, you know, for seeing and useful things like that."

"Officer Mills, may I?" Jacobs said.

"I've got this." He snapped.

I couldn't see him, given the fried state of my vision, but I heard the defensiveness in his voice. He wasn't happy. Wasn't happy with being partnered with Jacobs? Because she was a woman? Or because she was a couple of decades younger than him and more than likely better than him at his job. Pft, who was I kidding. A sponge would make a better police officer than Mills.

"I'm trained in First Aid." She replied, dulcet tones calm, "I need to assess the patient."

He didn't reply, but I heard a shuffling of feet and the movement of air near my face.

"Hi, Audrey, Officer Jacobs here. Are you hurt? Do you have any pain?"

I risked squinting open one eye, then after assessing it was safe for me to do so, the other one. "Nope. Just stuck. The seat belt is jammed." She crawled part way through the driver's side window, pushing the deflated airbag out of the way, and leaned around me to have a go at releasing the catch herself. "Stuck tight." She agreed, wriggling back out.

"You could just cut it loose." I suggested.

"Sorry, can't do that. You might have spinal injuries. I'm afraid you will have to stay where you are until the paramedics get here. Can you tell me what happened?"

The lie rolled right off my tongue. "I just took the corner too fast. I'm still getting used to driving this," I indicated the wreckage I was sitting in. "I guess with the higher center of gravity and all... I just tipped over."

One brow shot up, then lowered in a frown. "Excessive speed. You're going to get a ticket."

"That's the least of my problems." I said under my breath.

"What was that?"

"Nothing." I glanced around, wondering where Ben had gone. He could have told me it was the cops approaching and not the bad guys. Maybe it was payback for what I'd done to his car, but heck, it wasn't on purpose. My lie wasn't exactly a lie, excessive speed was most certainly a factor, I'd skidded around that corner on two wheels, hardly surprising the Nissan had rolled. But the reason I was speeding was not something I wanted to share with her.

The truth of it was I'd been surveilling a supposedly abandoned warehouse down by the docks when I'd been spotted. And the three guys who'd spotted me sported guns. I know this because they shot at me. And Ben had been yelling at me, telling me they had guns and to get out of there.

While I dangled upside down in my wrecked car waiting for the cavalry, Mills insisted on a sobriety test, which, shock upon shock, came up clean. Although Lord only knows I could use a drink now. The flash of blue and red lights had joined the headlights to light up the night sky, the police vehicle soon joined by an ambulance and then a fire truck.

"Audrey Fitzgerald, got yourself into another situation eh?" A head appeared at my window.

"Oh hi, Jace." I greeted the paramedic. "How you doing?"

"Yeah, I'm good. More importantly, how are you? Got any pain?" He pressed a gloved hand against my neck, checking my pulse. I shook my head, waited patiently while he shone yet another light in my eyes and did a quick but thorough inspection of my body. "Ned with you?" I asked conversationally. Jason grinned. "Sure is. Ned!" He called over his shoulder. "Collar." He held out his hand, and within seconds Ned had placed a cervical collar in his palm.

I groaned. "Do I really need that?"

"Just a precaution." He assured me, and really, I couldn't argue, not being stuck upside down like I was. After securing the collar around my neck, he told me, "I'm going to wriggle back out of this window and climb in the back seat so I'll be directly behind you. The rescue guys will pop the driver's side door off and release that seat belt and we're going to lower you, slowly, onto a spinal board and then slide you out of the car, okay?"

"Sure." There was a lot of activity, a lot of shouting and asking for equipment. The passenger door was wrenched open, as was the rear door. I could hear Jason climbing in, felt the vehicle rock with all the movement. My hand shot out to grab hold of something, anything, the sudden image of the car sliding down the hill on its roof popping into my head.

"Easy." Jason grabbed my flailing hand and gave it a squeeze. "You're okay."

I tried to nod, but with the collar wrapped around my neck, movement was difficult. "Can I ask you something?"

"Sure."

"When you guys arrived, were there any other vehicles around? Like maybe stopped further down the road? Did you pass anyone?" I asked.

"Not that I recall. Why?" He paused and I could practically hear the cogs turning in his head. "Was someone chasing you, Audrey? Is that why you had the accident?"

"Shh." I hissed. "I'm still in training and if I mess this up, if the FBPD get wind that I crashed because I was being pursued then Galloway may nix this whole PI thing and I'll be screwed." After all, Galloway had expressly asked me not to investigate the bank robbery. Only I'd ignored his request. He would not be pleased if he found out what had really happened.

"You'd rather they think you managed this on your own?" Jason's voice held just that right note of incredulity that told me he thought I was nuts.

"For now. After all, if you didn't see any other cars around, were they really chasing me?"

"What made you think they were?"

Gun fire. But I couldn't say that out loud, and to be honest I hadn't been concentrating on my rear-view mirror, just on getting my butt out of the docklands. Maybe they hadn't followed. And maybe finding myself parked on my roof was one hundred percent my fault. Although this would have to be at the very extreme scale of my clumsiness.

I didn't get a chance to answer though because suddenly it was a hive of activity. A firefighter had crawled into the passenger seat, a spinal board had been maneuvered into position, and then the seatbelt was cut. The sudden release of pressure was startling even though I knew it was coming I couldn't contain my gasp. "Easy." Jason murmured next to my ear as strong hands eased me down and then out the window.

I was sitting in the back of the ambulance when Galloway arrived, making a beeline straight for me.

"Audrey." He nodded in greeting and I couldn't tell if he was annoyed, relieved, concerned, or angry. Maybe all the above. "You okay?"

"I'm fine. Just a few scrapes and bruises." I assured him. "Jase. Tell him."

Jase winked at me before turning his attention to Galloway, "She's not lying." He confirmed. "Minor abrasions, some bruising from the seat belt."

"See?" I smiled. "I don't even need to go to hospital."

"You're going to hospital." Galloway and Jase said simultaneously.

"Hey!" I protested. "Quit ganging up on me."

"Audrey," Jase said with exaggerated patience. "We've talked about this. You could have internal injuries we're not aware of. I know I'm a pretty awesome paramedic, but even I don't have x-ray vision. And you, my girl, need x-rays and scans. At the very minimum."

"You're going to hospital." Galloway crossed his arms and planted his feet. I recognized the stance. It was something Ben used to do. What is it with alpha men always wanting to boss you around?

"Awww, isn't that sweet?" Ben cooed, appearing by Galloway's side. He'd made himself scarce throughout my rescue, but I figured he'd just been observing from the outside. Why sit in a mangled vehicle if you didn't have to? Ignoring Ben, I focused on Galloway. "As much as I enjoy having my frequent flyer card punched by the ER, because you know, after ten visits you get a free colonoscopy, I don't think it's fair to tie up vital resources unnecessarily."

"I thought you said it was a trip to Bermuda and steak knives?" Galloway's joke caught me by surprise.

"That too." I nodded. "But seriously, these guys

have checked me out and I've dodged a bullet, no ER today." I cringed at my turn of phrase.

"Nice try," Jase said, "but you're going. But I will compromise. You can come in the ambulance or make your own way there. And by that I mean someone else can drive you."

"Someone else?" I glanced toward Galloway. I still couldn't read his expression. He had a very good poker face.

"I'll take her." Galloway offered. Jase had known he would, for he had the nerve to fist bump him in front of me.

"It's not fair." I grumbled, but no one paid me any attention. Instead, I was bundled into Galloway's car, my protests ignored. Ben hitched a ride with us but remained mercifully silent the entire journey. I figured he was still miffed that I'd totaled his car. I wasn't thrilled with the situation myself, obviously.

To be fair, the trip to emergency went relatively smoothly. I had my frequent flyer card punched in the way of raised eyebrows and "you back again, Audrey?" type comments. I was poked, prodded, they drew blood to check I wasn't under the influence of drugs or alcohol, then I was sent off for scans and x-rays. Ben hung around the nurses' station, keeping one eye on me, the other on a brunette nurse.

I was lying on the gurney, pondering on how much to tell Galloway about the evening's events, when the doctor returned.

"How is she?" Galloway asked before I could get a word in.

"She will be fine. I've given her a thorough examination, her vitals are stable, she's not under the influence of drugs or alcohol, she has some soft tissue damage, some grazes that don't require sutures. No concussion. All in all she came out of this pretty lightly." The doctor then turned to me. "I suggest you take it easy for a few days. You will be sore, but nothing's broken and no internal bleeding."

I beamed while Galloway studied him intently for a moment before inclining his head ever so slightly. "So she's free to go?"

"Just need one signature on the release form and she's all yours." The doctor handed me a clipboard and pointed to the bottom where I dutifully signed.

Sliding down from the gurney, I gave the doctor and nurses a wave. "Thanks guys, no offense but I hope I don't see you soon!"

5

The car ride home was frosty. Ben made himself comfortable in the back seat. Now that he knew I was okay, he launched into berating me over what had happened to his car before eventually running out of steam and lapsing into merciful silence. Galloway hadn't said a word, though by the way his fingers clenched the steering wheel I suspected he had a lot of words he wanted to say. I was grateful he was keeping them to himself. It had been one hell of a day, and exhaustion was licking at my heels.

Pulling up out the front of Ben's house, Galloway killed the engine, rested one arm on the steering wheel and turned to face me.

"Care to tell me what really happened?"

"Okay, look, I know I was going too fast. It was stupid and reckless of me, I totally own that and I'm sorry."

"Oh, I know you were speeding, Audrey. I want to know why you were speeding."

I turned my attention to the windscreen, staring at the dark street. I guess I should have told him I hadn't moved into Ben's house yet, that I'd chickened out and was still in my apartment, but for some reason I'd kept my mouth shut. Maybe it was because of the waves of anger I could feel emanating from him? Maybe it was my own sense of self-preservation kicking in. Plus, it wouldn't hurt to spend the night at Ben's. Having Thor curl into my side to keep me company sounded strangely comforting.

"Audrey." Galloway growled, "I'm this close to losing my cool with you." I snuck a glance and saw him hold up his finger and thumb, demonstrating how close he was to losing his patience. I bit my lip. I didn't like him being angry with me and I knew if I told him the truth he'd be furious. But the truth was, I'd found the warehouse the bank robbers were using. Well, Ben and I had. Because I'd had the brilliant idea of heading to the wharf and warehouse district and sending Ben on a reconnaissance mission. He hadn't found the white van, but he had found discarded clown masks in an old warehouse.

I'd settled in to wait for them to return, my first ever stakeout. As exciting as it was, it was also terrifying when I'd slipped on gravel when trying to peek through a side window. Of course they'd heard me. Of course they'd busted out their guns and come after me. Of course I totally panicked and lost control of my vehicle.

"Just tell him, Fitz." Ben sighed from the backseat.

"I can't." I whispered. He'd be mad, rightly so, and I faced the genuine possibility that he'd cancel our arrangement and no longer be my supervisor. And if I didn't have a supervisor, I couldn't finish my PI training and if I didn't have my PI license, I couldn't run Delaney Investigations. My heart ached at the thought. I had to keep it going. It was the one way I had of keeping Ben's memory alive. Not that it was a major issue for me, I got to see his ghostly hide every single day, but that wasn't the point.

"Why?" Galloway's voice was as rough as nails and I chanced a look at his face. Yep. Pissed didn't cover it.

I sniffed. "You're going to be mad."

"In case it's escaped your attention, I'm already mad."

To my utter horror, my eyes welled with tears. *No!* No, don't you dare cry, Audrey Fitzgerald, I scolded myself. Do not turn on the tears. You are stronger than this. You can handle an angry cop. Seems my eyeballs didn't get the memo for a big fat tear overflowed, promptly followed by another.

"Jesus." Galloway swore, slamming his fist on the steering wheel, making me jump. I fumbled for the door catch and slid out of the car, bolting for the front door.

With each step my side ached where the seatbelt had dug in, but I ignored the twinge, hustling as fast as I could. I hated to cry. And I hated having witnesses when I did even more. Sniffing, I felt in my pockets for my keys, doing a frantic pat down when I realized I didn't have them. I stopped cold and stared up at the starlight sky in resigned disbelief. Of course I didn't have them. They were dangling from the ignition of Ben's totaled Nissan. Another tear fell, and I angrily wiped it away.

The sound of a car door slamming jolted me out of my self pity. Fine. I'd just find another way inside. Pivoting, I headed toward the side of the house. Hearing footsteps behind me, I picked up the pace.

"Audrey. Wait." There was a world of emotion in his voice. Anger. Frustration. And something else I couldn't put my finger on. But one thing I knew was that I wanted to be alone, for an emotional tsunami was bearing down on me and I did not want any witnesses when it hit. Rather than slow my pace, I was practically jogging when I skidded around the rear corner of the house. Moonlight spilled over the deck, lighting my way. I don't know what I was planning, that maybe I could wriggle through the cat door, but it needn't have mattered for my wrist was seized in a steely grip and Galloway ground out, "would you just wait!?"

I turned on him. "Why?" I yelled, startling us both. "So you can yell at me some more? About how stupid I was? How reckless? You think I don't know that? You think I don't feel awful that I totaled Ben's car and could have killed myself in the process? I guess you're done with me now, huh? I guess this is it for you, you can't continue to be my supervisor."

"Is that what you think? That I'm going to bail on you?"

"Aren't you?" I challenged.

"No." He still had a firm grip on my wrist but I

stopped resisting and stood there, staring at him, mouth agape.

"You aren't?" The pesky tears filled my eyes again and all I could see was a blur, so when a rough thumb scraped across my cheek to wipe a tear away I jumped.

"Audrey Fitzgerald, you do my head in." He whispered, stepping closer to rest his forehead against mine. I froze. Being this close to him was divine torture.

"In a good way, of course." I joked, not sure what to make of this current situation. The corners of his mouth tugged into a devilish grin. "In all the ways." He whispered.

A wicked heat wound through my body, along with a little hum of pleasure. The hand that had been wrapped around my wrist now slid up my arm, across my shoulder and behind my neck, every stroke of his fingers spiraled right down to my toes as he sensually massaged my nape before sliding along my jawline to tilt my head back.

I gazed into his eyes before my own fluttered shut as his face moved closer. His breath was hot on my face a second before his mouth covered mine. I'm pretty sure the earth stopped turning at that point and gravity failed as I floated up into the sky. I leaned into him, wrapping my arms around his neck, ignoring the twinges and aches in my battered body as a new ache took up residence. His kiss was everything and more. Hot and hard, yet sweet and gentle.

And then something clicked in my brain. I was kissing a cop. *A cop!* Hell of a time for that pesky thought to surface, but once it appeared I couldn't push it down, couldn't ignore it. All my distrust raced to the surface, and I stiffened, panic sweeping through me. As sexy as I found Captain Cowboy Hot Pants, we shouldn't be doing this. Despite me pining desperately for a date for the last few weeks now he'd finally made a move? I panicked. Breaking the kiss, I pushed away from him.

"It's too soon. You're not ready." Galloway's voice was low, rough, laced with one hundred layers of emotion. I shook my head. No. For as much as I lusted after this very fine specimen of manhood currently standing in front of me, he was right. Now was not the time. I was a mass of contradicting emotion, not to mention physical pain.

He ran a finger over my cheek and blew out a breath. "Balls in your court, Fitz. I won't push but I know you feel it too... we have a connection. I'll be here when you're ready." I blinked, at a loss for words, not sure what to say or what to do.

"Ahem." Thor cleared his throat from behind me. "Are you finished?"

I never thought I'd welcome a cat's interruption, but now it seemed Thor's appearance was divine intervention. I leaned down to run my hand over his fur, buying time to regain my composure.

"Guess he must be hungry." Galloway commented, leaning around me to look at the meowing Thor.

"That's a given. There's never a time when he's not." I had to bite my lip to keep from saying more.

"If you've finished sucking face," Thor huffed, "perhaps we can go inside. It's rare I see you at this time of day." His words triggered a wave of guilt and I realized that despite Thor's insistence that he was fine spending nights on his own, perhaps he wasn't being entirely truthful.

Galloway turned toward the deck. "Let's go inside and you can tell me exactly what happened, and then you need to get some rest. Hurt or not, you were just in a car accident and I suspect the adrenalin rush has well and truly worn off."

I blinked in surprise. That was it? No more talking about feelings and emotions and that kiss?

That one that had just rocked my world. That same one where I'd pushed him away? Fine. That was exactly what I wanted. I think.

Putting on my game face, I straightened my spine and nodded. "Don't suppose you have my keys by any chance?" I rolled my shoulders and began the monumental effort of climbing the three back steps. Every cell in my body ached. They'd clearly got the memo—en masse—that it was time to hurt, and every muscle and nerve ending joined in with great gusto. Hiding the grimace, I heaved myself up, my hips and pelvis protesting the loudest. I was in a sweat by the time I reached the sliding glass door.

A jingle of keys caught my attention, and I shuffled around to see Galloway holding a set of keys aloft. I squinted, peering closer. "Are those mine?"

"They are. If you hadn't bolted out of the car, I would have given them to you. And your phone." He climbed the stairs with ease and handed me the keys, waited patiently while I took an inordinate amount of time unlocking the door because my fingers were refusing to behave.

"Need a hand?" His breath was hot in my ear, and I shivered. Ordinarily I'd baulk at the idea of needing a man, let alone a cop, help me open my door, but now was not the time for foolish pride, for my legs were rapidly turning into overcooked noodles and I feared I'd be reduced to crawling over the threshold any second.

"Yes, please."

He didn't say a word, just closed his big hand over mine, guided the key into the lock and turned. My arm dropped to my side, and he slid the door open, the heat of him behind me a comfort, but I couldn't lean back and bask in it, not if I didn't want to end up in a puddle at his feet, so I pushed myself forward, shuffling toward the sofa. I made it just in time, flopping face down along the length while Galloway flicked on the lights. Closing my eyes, I listened as he pottered around in the kitchen. I heard kibble being poured into a bowl and his deep voice talking softly to Thor; I heard the coffee machine fire up—that was almost enough for me to poke my head up... almost. I lay there on my stomach, one arm dangling, and watched Ben, who was sprawled on the sofa opposite.

"Hurts huh?" He said sympathetically. I nodded. Just a tad. But I trusted what the hospital had told me. Soft tissue damage, which meant there was nothing they could do other than administer pain relief. And I also knew Galloway had been right. The adrenaline rush I'd had from fleeing the bad guys and then flipping my car had worn off, unmasking the pain waiting to hit me. My wobbly emotions were still wobbly, but my aching muscles had taken the focus away and for that I was grateful.

"You should tell him the truth." Ben cocked his head, indicating Galloway. "He might be mad but that's not the worst of your problems."

"I'm scared he'll quit being my supervisor." I whispered. Understanding dawned on Ben's face, "Ahhh. Look, he's a good guy, Fitz. He won't bail on you. And this wasn't your fault—it was mine. I should have known better. But it seemed a good idea at the time, searching the warehouses for the van. I was caught up in the excitement of it, just like you were, forgetting that you don't have the experience. I put you in a dangerous situation and I'm sorry."

"Forgiven." I tried to smile but only one half of my mouth obeyed, quirking up in more of a sneer than a grin.

A steaming cup of coffee appeared on the coffee table in front of me, along with a glass of water. Pushing myself upright, I swung my legs to the floor and watched in horror as Galloway sat on Ben. My mouth opened to warn him and my hand reached out as Ben floated up through Galloway to stand to one side. Galloway shivered, muttered, "someone just walked over my grave." Then his gray eyes turned in my direction. Leaning forward, he held out a hand. "Take these. Then tell me exactly what happened."

*a*fter swallowing the painkillers I took a sip of the coffee, buying time, trying to figure out how much to tell Galloway. How do you explain to a cop that your ghost friend was materializing through walls to search for the van the bank robbers had used without sounding certifiable? Short answer, you didn't.

"How's your case going?" I asked instead.

"My case?" One eyebrow arched.

"Corruption in the force? I see Mills is still on the payroll." I said the last with a grumble. It turns out, before Ben had died he'd agreed to help Galloway with a secret internal investigation into corruption within the Firefly Bay Police Department. Only Ben hadn't had the chance to give Galloway any of the evidence he'd collected from when he'd been forced out of the job he loved—fighting crime and bringing criminals to justice—by liars and cheats within the force. My stance towards cops had softened somewhat when Galloway had told me of the investigation and his determination to bring down the corrupt officials who'd made Ben's life hell.

Galloway took a sip of his own coffee. "Slow going. I have to be careful I don't tip anyone off. This isn't just about Mills, he's small fry. This goes higher up the food chain and I need to find out if it's all the way to the top before I make a move."

"All the way to the top? You think Police Chief Hart could be corrupt?" I don't know why I was surprised. Galloway told me when I'd handed over Ben's files that he thought it was integrated deeply in the Firefly Bay Force and if that meant the top dog was corrupt then Galloway would have a hell of a job proving it.

Galloway shrugged. "Anything is possible. Now enough deflecting. Time to talk. What happened tonight?"

Knowing I was out of time, I answered in a rush, my words running together. "After the hold up today, I figured I'd go down to Driftwood Landing to check out the warehouses. They ditched our phones in the wharf district so I figured they probably hid the van there somewhere so it couldn't hurt to have a look around." To give him credit, Galloway didn't react like I thought he would. I'd been expecting an eye roll—as if the cops hadn't already searched the area. Or berate me for sticking my nose into a police investigation. He did neither of those things, merely took a sip of coffee, then asked, "and? Did you find the van?"

"I didn't." I shook my head. "But I found something else. Clown masks in one of the warehouses." To be honest, it was Ben who'd found the masks, but Galloway didn't need to know that.

"Clown masks?" He straightened and placed his coffee on the table, leaning forward to rest his forearms on his knees.

"I know, right? What are the odds that someone happens to have clown masks lying around in their warehouse the day a bank robbery takes place where the perpetrators are wearing clown masks? I figured it couldn't be a coincidence, so I waited to see if they'd come back." A slight surge of adrenaline rushed through me at the memory.

"But you didn't see the van?"

Shaking my head, I continued, "not from my vantage point."

"Which was?"

"Side window."

His eyes narrowed. "So you were poking around down at the docklands, peering in through windows, and no one stopped you?"

"No one saw me." I corrected, "I was being discreet. Plus, I figured the robbers probably weren't there. If it were me I'd have hidden the van, ditched the phones, gone to my day job or whatever to establish alibis should any suspicion come my way."

He leaned back against the sofa and crossed his arms across his chest. "Then what? You settled in to wait all afternoon? On the off chance they'd return?"

"Yes."

"And they did. This evening." He prodded.

"Yep. I was in my car, parked up in the lot, but I could see the warehouse in question. When a car rolled in just after dark, I snuck down to look through the window again. Only I slipped on the gravel and fell against the siding, making a noise."

"Ah. They heard you." He nodded, putting together the pieces before I got the story out.

"They did."

"So...?"

"I ran."

"Why run? Why not hide?"

He would not be happy with this next part, and I screwed my face up in anticipation. "They had guns."

Kudos to him, he stayed remarkably calm. "You saw the guns? How many men?"

"Three men. And I kinda saw the guns."

"Kinda?"

"Well, they were shooting at me, so I figured they had guns."

"Shooting at you?!" His voice went up, and he jumped to his feet, startling me. I pressed back against the sofa, chewing my lip. Here it came. He would be all sorts of mad. I watched while he raised his eyes to the ceiling and appeared to count to ten. Then he blew out a breath and resumed his seat.

"Let me make sure I've got this straight. You spent the day peeking through windows at Driftwood Landing. Then, upon your discovery of clown masks, you staked out a warehouse for several hours, until the suspects returned. By then it was nightfall. Only you were discovered, and they opened fire. I'm assuming what happened next was that you successfully returned to your car and sped out of there—with them chasing you. You said they returned to the warehouse in a car. Not a van?"

"No, not a van. A sedan. A dark one. It could have been black, but since it was night, I really couldn't tell, it may have been blue or gray, but definitely a dark color."

"And did they give chase?"

I paused, thinking back to the events of earlier this evening. They'd opened fire, taking shots at me through the warehouse siding. I'd sprinted to the car with Ben yelling at me the entire time. I'd been in panic mode. I'd sped out of the parking lot with wheels spinning and gravel flying. I'd seen light spilling out from the warehouse doors in my rearview mirror, but had I seen headlights behind me? I'd thought they'd been chasing me, but I couldn't be one hundred percent certain.

"I thought they were." I told Galloway. "But I'll be honest once I was behind the wheel I was focusing on driving and getting the hell out of there." I let my eyes drift from Galloway to Ben, who was leaning against the wall just behind Galloway's left shoulder. He shrugged. "I was too preoccupied with your maniac driving to look behind us." He said. But they hadn't been behind me when I'd rolled the Nissan, otherwise I'd be sitting here with a bullet in my head. Which meant they'd given up the chase sometime beforehand. But why?

Galloway read my mind. "At some point they ended the chase. Probably realized that you'd report the shooting, that you could have been on the phone to the police during the chase, they'd have returned to the warehouse to destroy evidence."

I sat forward, wincing at the protesting of my bruised flesh. "We need to get to Driftwood Landing, to the warehouse."

"Nuh uh. You aren't going anywhere. It's time to hand this one over to us—which is what you should have done in the first place." He let that sink in. "Which warehouse was it?"

I gave him the information he needed and showed him the photos I'd snapped that afternoon of the view from the window. You could just make out the clown masks on a workbench, almost out of shot. Galloway examined them closely, then looked at me. "You must have exceptional vision," he said. "If you hadn't told me they were clown masks, I wouldn't have picked it."

I shrugged. Same. Cradling my coffee cup, I watched Captain Cowboy Hot Pants from beneath my lashes, my eyes lingering on his lips. That kiss. I sighed, remembering the feel of his mouth on mine, the brush of his tongue, the taste of him, the way my toes curled and heat swirled through me. And then the panic returned, squashing those warm fuzzy feelings into cold hard terror. Despite knowing I could trust Galloway, some part of me wasn't one hundred percent convinced kissing him had been a good idea.

Galloway stood. "Get some rest, Audrey. I'll check on you later." Carrying his cup to the sink, he washed it, dried it, and put it away.

"Pft, I'm fine." I assured him from my position on the couch. It was a total lie, of course. My body felt like it had gone ten rounds with Mike Tyson and I wasn't sure I could actually stand at this point.

"Sure." He grinned, then let himself out the back door with a wave. I listened as his footsteps faded and the house settled into silence once more.

"Sorry, Audrey." Ben sprawled on the sofa opposite me. "I got us into this. It's my fault, not yours."

"You're right." I agreed, "It is totally your fault. But how awesome was today?"

He frowned. "Awesome? Do you have a concussion?"

I shook my head, holding up one hand as I ticked off on my fingers. "Involved in a bank robbery, conducted my first stake out and my first car chase."

Ben chuckled. "I'm not sure the car chase counts when it's you being chased." He pointed out. Fair call, but still, it highlighted something. "I need more training."

"You certainly need to get a gun license." Ben agreed. I'd never given much thought to guns before, I wasn't for or against them, they'd just never factored into my life but now I couldn't help but agree. Today could have turned out differently if I'd been armed. But my concern that I'd accidentally shoot myself was valid.

"And defensive driving training. I should be able to take a corner, at speed, and not roll."

"Car chases are not a big component of being a PI." Ben pointed out.

"Yet here we are." I argued. "Your car is written off. And I've only been a PI for a few weeks."

"PI in training." He pointed out.

I brushed him off. "Semantics." Just then my stomach grumbled, reminding me I had eaten nothing other than the bag of crisps I'd found discarded in Ben's car during the stakeout. The painkillers had kicked in and I was feeling semi-human again. Pushing to my feet, I shuffled to the fridge and flung it open.

"Bugger." It was empty. Of course it was, I scolded myself, no-one lived here, why would there be food in the fridge? I turned my attention to the pantry. "Bingo!"

Ten minutes later I was staring at a steaming plate of Annie's Mac & Cheese.

"Would be better if you added butter." Ben leaned over the plate to take a sniff.

"Yeah well, no butter here, so I'll have to make do. Surprised you even had this in your pantry."

"Pays to have emergency rations."

"I'm not sure this classifies as an emergency, but whatever, I'm just glad you have food." I blew on the plate, practically drooling as the aroma of the cheese filled my nostrils. Scooping my fork into the macaroni goodness, I shoveled it into my mouth, ignoring the searing heat as I chewed and swallowed. "So good." Scoop, chew, swallow, on repeat until I scraped the plate clean.

"You were hungry!" Ben said.

"Yup." Pushing back my chair, I stood, reached to pick up my plate only I didn't get a good grip, and it crashed to the floor, smashing into pieces. I yelped and jumped back, thankful none of the shards got me.

"Just leave it, Fitz. Sweep it up in the morning. You're dead on your feet and you'll probably end up slicing open a finger if you attempt to clean it up tonight."

I looked from my dead friend to the broken plate on the floor and as much as it pained me to leave it, he was right. I wasn't even sure I could bend over to clean it up, anyway. "Thor won't cut himself on it, will he?"

"I'm not an imbecile." Thor sniffed from his spot on an armchair.

"Sorry, sorry, you're right. Just be careful, don't walk around here. If you get a sliver in your paw, then I'm taking you to the vet." I eyeballed the cat, knowing how he felt about the vet. Not a fan was putting it mildly.

7

*T*here was an insistent voice in my ear yelling, "wake up!" Instead I rolled over, tucking the covers up over my ears to block out the noise.

"Audrey!" Ben insisted. I played possum, pretending I hadn't heard him. If I ignored him long enough, maybe—hopefully—he'd go away. "You try." I heard him say, then felt the weight of a four legged body as it walked along the length of me until it was balanced precariously along my upper arm, paws digging in. I'd have bruises for sure. Thor lowered his head to my ear and said, "you're on telly."

I sat up in a flash, sending the cat flying. I caught sight of him as he trotted out the door, tail aloft, saying to Ben as he passed. "You're welcome."

"What do you mean, I'm on telly?" I called after him. Flinging the covers back, I swung my legs out of bed and groaned as my muscles screamed in protest.

"He means television." Ben said, hopping from foot to foot in some mad ghostly shuffle of excitement.

I rolled my eyes, "I know that much." Duh. "I meant, why am I on television? And how do you know that?" Still wearing the same clothes from yesterday, I padded into the living room and picked up the remote.

"News channel." Ben said, brushing past me and sending an icy shiver down my arm. "I was two doors down, watching the morning news." He explained. Since Ben couldn't turn on the television himself, he'd worked out a system of visiting different homes in the neighborhood until he found one with the television on, and he'd hunker down and watch whatever was on, all without the hapless neighbor knowing they were being haunted.

"The bank robbery?" I guessed, flicking through the channels until I reached the local news. Sure enough, my photo was on the screen behind the presenter. "Why do they have a photo of me?"

Ben shrugged, eyes glued to the screen, "Dunno.

They led with it. Local PI caught up in a bank heist." He air quoted. I frowned, curious why no-one had contacted me for an interview, or even a quote.

"Your phone's dead by the way." Ben told me, pointing to where I'd left my phone on the coffee table the night before. Correction. Galloway had retrieved it from the car wreck. I vaguely remember him telling me, but I was pretty zonked by that time. Of course my charger was back in my apartment.

I nodded. "That explains why they didn't contact me for my side of the story." I said. "Good publicity though."

The news report on the bank robbery ended, no mention of me totaling my car while fleeing from who I assumed were the bank robbers. Thank God.

"Local psychic Madam Myra was found dead in her shop this morning—" the news anchor read from the teleprompter. "Police confirmed foul play and anyone with any information is asked to contact the Firefly Bay Police Department." Footage flashed on the screen of a crowd gathered around the outside of the psychic's shop, Nether & Void. I spotted Galloway and peered closer. "Is that?" I blinked, then rubbed my eyes to clear my vision. "Is Galloway talking with Jacob Henry?"

"Who?" Ben asked, moving closer to the television, following my pointing finger.

"That guy." I stepped up to the screen and jabbed a finger at the young man. It was definitely Jacob Henry, the teller from the Firefly Bay Community Bank, I was sure of it.

"Looks like he discovered the body." Ben said, crossing his arms and watching the scene that had obviously been recorded on someone's phone, given the amount of camera shake going on. Looks like they'd zoomed in too, the picture was that grainy.

"I'm going down there." I declared, quickly running my fingers through my hair, ignoring the twinge in my shoulders and neck when I raised my arms.

"Breakfast first." Thor demanded, sitting in front of his food bowl. I still hadn't replaced the cereal bowl I'd been using as a temporary measure, despite Ben constantly reminding me that human bowls were not meant for pets. I failed to see the problem with it, but it really made Ben twitchy and I admit that was probably why I forgot to buy Thor a new bowl, some days it was fun to see Ben squirm.

After feeding Thor and clearing up the smashed plate from the night before, I smoothed down the wrinkled clothes I'd slept in and headed out the door.

The screaming was coming from inside Nether & Void, and it was relentless. An ongoing wail that hurt my ears. "What is that noise?" I glanced around at the handful of bystanders who'd lingered on after the police had left, yet none of them seemed concerned about the blaring racket coming from Nether & Void.

"What noise? I don't hear anything—except for the waves." A teenager in ripped jeans and tie dye T-shirt replied, indicating the wooden platform we were standing on and the ocean gently ebbing and flowing beneath. There were five boutique shops running the length of the boardwalk, with a large cafe at the end. Nether & Void was nestled in between a new aged shop called Nine, and a tattoo parlor called Inkognito.

"Are you saying no-one else can hear that?" I waved a hand at the door, the wailing continuing from inside. What was it, some sort of alarm?

"Lady, you're nuts." The teenager spun on her heel and ambled away, apparently having lost interest now the police had gone. I eyed the back of her tie dye t-shirt, wondering if they were coming back into fashion or if she'd found it in a charity store. I made a mental note to investigate further... I could definitely see a tie dye T-shirt in my future.

A woman with long blonde dreadlocks, a black tank top that showcased a full sleeve of mandala tattoos, enough bracelets around one wrist to qualify as weight lifting, and a long, bright, floral skirt that brushed her ankles appeared in the doorway of Nine and gasped. "You're her!" I glanced around to see who she was referring to, stumbled backward when she hurried toward me, grabbing my arm. "I saw you on the news! You're that private investigator."

I blushed. "Oh, yeah," clearing my throat, I threw out a fake smile. "That's me." I wasn't used to being recognized, but now that I'd had my face plastered over the television, I guess I'd better get used to it.

"I want to hire you," she said over her shoulder as she tugged on my arm, giving me no option but to follow. Inside her store I was greeted with softly playing new age music and the distinct smell of incense. The shelves were stacked with books, jewelry, crystals, candles and oils, and in one corner a rack of clothing.

"My name's Ashley," she turned, releasing my

wrist. "Ashley Baker. I own Nine. And Myra was my neighbor and friend."

"Right." I nodded.

"And I want you to find out who did this to her." Ashley continued.

"I charge a fee." I blurted. Smooth Audrey, smooth.

She waved a hand, "Money's no problem. Where do we start? And what's wrong with your shoulder?" I paused where I'd been absently massaging my aching shoulder, quickly dropping my hand. "Nothing. So tell me about Myra. How long have you known her? You said you were friends, do you mean friends outside of being shop neighbors, or work friends?"

The wailing sound from the other side of the wall intensified, and I frowned. "Are you sure you can't hear that?"

Ashley looked from me to the wall and back again, before crossing to the counter and rummaging behind it. She handed me a crystal. "Here. This might help. Your aura is all off. And there's something wrong with your body."

I jerked my head back. "What?" How rude!

"You're carrying yourself as if you're in pain." Ashley explained. "Nine stands for the nine senses;

sight, sound, taste, smell, touch, temperature, pain, balance, and body awareness. It's my job to help my customers experience good health, happiness, and harmony."

"I thought there were only five senses." I looked at the crystal resting on my palm. I'd never really believed all this new age stuff but considering I could now see ghosts and talk to cats who was I to diss it?

"That's what most people think, but there's so much more. Let me give you a massage on the house, while I tell you about Myra. It'll help with your pain." She added when I hesitated.

"You massage as well?"

She pointed to a door at the back of the store. "I have a private room there. I also run meditation classes—you should come, you seem awfully tense."

"I'll pass on the meditation thanks." I'd tried it before, but I could never get my mind to shut up long enough to get any real benefit. "But I'll accept the massage." I handed the crystal back to her only it slipped from my fingers and bounced to the floor. "Sorry. Do you have anything that can help with clumsiness?" I added, doing my best not to groan as I bent and scooped the crystal from the floor.

"Actually, I do. Come." Her long skirt swished

around her legs and her bracelets jangled as she strode to the closed door at the rear of her shop. Holding it open, she waited for me to pass through. "I'm going to make up a mixture of Ember Petal and Sogo Grass oils for your massage. While I do that, you can get undressed and make yourself comfortable on the table—cover yourself with the towel." She'd closed the door before I could respond. With a shrug, I toed off my shoes and had shimmied out of my jeans when Ben walked through the wall from next door.

"Ben!" I hissed, clutching my jeans to my hips. "What are you doing here?"

"I know what that sound is." He said, glancing around the room that was totally dominated by a massage table draped in violet towels.

"Oh?" that caught my attention. "So you can hear it? I thought I was going crazy."

He smirked, shaking his head. "You? Crazy? Pft." Then he crossed his eyes and twirled his finger at his temple.

"Ha, ha. Look, I'm about to get a massage and find out all about Myra, the psychic who was killed, so make it quick."

"That sound? Is a woman screaming."

"What woman? Who?"

"Myra Hansen."

"The dead psychic?"

"The one and only."

"And I can hear her because..." I knew it. I knew what was coming, it was approaching like a freight train, bearing down on me and I was stuck, like a deer in the headlights, paralyzed, unable to move.

"She's a ghost." He confirmed.

The door opened, and Ashley poked her head in. "All set?" Seeing me standing there clutching my jeans to my hips, she blinked in surprise. "Oh. Sorry. I'll give you a few more minutes," and closed the door again.

My head was spinning, and I needed time to process. "Can you get out!" I hissed, waving Ben away. "Go talk to her, calm her down. I'll meet you out front once I've finished here."

"Sure." Ben winked and stepped back through the wall to the wailing ghost next door. Shaking my head, I tossed the jeans onto the chair provided and pulled my t-shirt over my head, quickly followed by my bra before sliding beneath the towel on the table. "I'm ready." I called out. The door opened immediately, and Ashley came into the room, carrying a small brown bottle with her. "So I've made you up a special mixture of oils," she said, busying herself behind me, "Ember Petal is for healing, and Sogo Grass which is for balancing." I watched over my shoulder as she removed the bracelets and placed them next to the bottle of oil, then expertly twisted her waist length dreadlocks up into a loose bun and secured them with a scrunchie.

"Sounds good." I said, placing my face in the hole in the massage table and looking at the floor beneath us. "Will this take long?"

"Not long at all, I'll keep it brief as I'm the only one in the store today. I locked the door so we won't be disturbed but I'm keen to open again as quickly as possible since I'm betting we'll get a lot of sticky beaks down here today wanting to know what happened at Nether & Void."

"What did happen?" I asked.

Ashley folded the towel covering me down to my hips, exposing my back. I heard her startled breath.

"What?" I lifted my head to stare at her over my shoulder.

"You have some magnificent bruises here." She gently touched my shoulder and ribs. "How did this happen?"

"Car accident." I lowered my head back into position. "It's all good, just soft tissue damage, nothing to worry about."

"I should have added more Ember Petal." She muttered, then began gently kneading the oil into my flesh.

"Relax." She said. Easy for her to say. I wasn't one for relaxing, wasn't one for having strangers touch me, but desperate times called for desperate measures. "Tell me about Myra." I invited, all the while processing the disturbing news that I could hear Myra, crying for want of a better word, next door. Did that mean I'd be able to see her, talk to her, like I did Ben? I wasn't prepared for this. I thought I had a connection with Ben because we were best friends and that explained why I could communicate with him. But Myra was a stranger to me. How was this even possible?

"We met a few months ago when Myra leased the shop next door." Ashley's words interrupted my musings, and I temporarily shelved them and listened to what she had to say. "We clicked immediately and were soon lunch buddies, closing up our stores and having our breaks at the Seaview Cafe." The Seaview Cafe was the huge restaurant come cafe at the end of the boardwalk, popular among tourists and locals alike. "She's a few years older than me," Ashley continued, "but it didn't make a difference. Myra said age shouldn't be judged by a number. I guess considering her boyfriend is so much older than her she didn't like people making judgements about age."

"How old is her boyfriend?"

"She's thirty-three, he's fifty-one. It's so sad you know, her dying, because I think Lee was about to propose."

"Oh?"

"Mmmm. Myra was saying they had big plans, that things would change and that she was really excited about it, that she was just waiting on Lee."

"Were you friends outside of work? Did you see each other socially?" I asked through a groan as her supple fingers massaged my aching muscles. She was good, the tight muscles giving way to her expert touch. The aroma of the oils wasn't half bad either.

"Nah, not really. But since we're both here almost six days a week, we saw each other plenty."

"What do you know about her clients? Was she having trouble with anyone?"

"A lot of her clients are one-offs. Tourists who come in for a Tarot reading, that type of thing. She has a couple of regulars I've seen coming and going frequently. That Regina Davis," Ashley snorted, "this woman is so rich and yet here she is, visiting Myra to talk to her dead poodle. Can you believe it?"

"You're not a believer then?" I grunted.

"Oh, I believe. How could I not? But not in communicating with your pets beyond the veil."

"So what do you think about Myra providing that service for her?" I pushed. "If you don't believe that is a thing, was Myra ripping her off?"

Ashley's hands paused. "Interesting question." She began kneading again. "I hadn't really thought about it that way before."

"Any other clients you know about?"

"Just that guy who found her. He's been visiting solidly for weeks now. Almost daily."

"Jacob Henry?"

"I don't know his name. Myra told me she had a golden ticket of a client, I assumed it was him or Regina, they were her only regulars that I know of, everyone else was a walk in."

I lapsed into silence, digesting what she'd told me. I'd hardly consider Jacob Henry a golden ticket of a client, not on a bank teller's wage, but maybe he had family money, or his wife had money. But then if he was visiting Myra daily, the cost of those visits would be mounting. I made a mental note to check him out.

8

*L*eaning my elbows against the railing and staring out to sea, I ignored the alarming spectacle of Ben hovering above the ocean in front of me. Using my phone as a decoy, I pressed it to my ear so we could talk without me looking like I was talking to myself and labeled certifiable. It worked well unless my phone actually rang.

"You smell nice." Ben grinned. He was right. The oils Ashley had used in my massage had me not only feeling wonderful, but smelling pretty darn good as well. We'd been ignoring the wailing that continued from inside Nether & Void. Myra Hansen was clearly distraught at her death, but until she quit screaming about it, there wasn't much I could do. "Did she say anything? Anything at all?" I asked Ben, jerking my head toward the source of the irritating sound.

"Nope. She's sitting at her table with her head in her hands, wailing."

I turned, eyeing the police tape across the door. No way I could get into the store and see for myself, I'd have to get Ben to coax her out. "Did you tell her I can see ghosts?" I asked, ignoring the startled look of a passerby who'd overheard me.

"I did, but I don't think she can hear anything over her own noise."

"Damn it. I really need to get in there and speak with her. I have a feeling she isn't going to quit until I do, she's been wailing nonstop for over an hour now." I eyed Nine, the shop next door. Ashley said she was good friends with Myra. Good enough to have a spare key to her store? Sliding the phone into my back pocket, I headed back to Nine, the bell above the door tinkling as I pushed it open. Ashley glanced up from the counter where she was flicking through a catalogue. "Oh, hey. Back so soon?"

"You wouldn't happen to have a key to next door would you? You and Myra didn't keep a spare for each other?"

Ashley reached beneath the counter and produced a silver keyring, dangling it in the air. "Of course we do. But... isn't it a crime scene? Are you allowed to go in?"

I accepted the key and grinned. "I won't tell if you won't."

Back outside, unable to believe my luck, I approached the door to Nether & Void. "Keep an eye out, will you?" I whispered to Ben who was hovering by my shoulder. "And this time I mean, really keep an eye out."

"Okay, okay." He grumbled, remembering the last time I'd asked him to keep a lookout and he'd failed miserably, too excited in joining me in investigating that we'd nearly gotten caught somewhere we shouldn't have been. Correction. I nearly got caught. He was a ghost. It wasn't an issue for him.

Turning the key in the lock, I pushed the door open, ducking beneath the police tape before quietly closing the door behind me. So far, so good. Ben stepped through and joined me.

Sure enough, sitting at the small round table draped in a black tablecloth hunched the figure of a woman, cradling her head in her hands and screaming. It was louder now that I was in the room with her, setting my teeth on edge. And one other thing. It was now confirmed I could see dead people. I'd thought seeing Ben was some sort of anomaly but

Myra Hansen with her boho chic blouse and black leather pants—at least I think they were leather from what I could see of one leg poking out from under the table—was most definitely a ghost and I could most definitely see her.

"I don't believe this." I could see ghosts. Not just Ben, but ghosts. Plural. How had this even happened? I'd never really questioned it before, but now I was curious, for sitting before me, looking as real and alive as the nose on my face, was one recently murdered—and understandably upset—psychic. She clearly hadn't seen this coming.

"Who are you?" Myra lifted her head, her nose red, her hair a wild riot of curls where they'd escaped from the colorful scarf tied around her head. At least she'd stopped wailing.

Sliding into the chair opposite her I replied, "I'm Audrey Fitzgerald, I'm a private investigator." I cocked my head toward Ben, "and this is Ben Delaney."

"And... and... I'm dead?" her chin wobbled, and a big fat tear rolled down her cheek. Curious. I didn't think ghosts could cry. I watched in fascination as the tear rolled down her face, reached her jawline and dripped off, disappearing into the ether.

"I'm afraid so."

Myra's watery eyes landed on Ben. "And you? You're a ghost? Like me?"

"Yup." Ben nodded. "It's not so bad." He patted her on the back awkwardly, well tried to, but two ghosts touching? Wasn't going to work. Instead, a cloud of mist appeared where two separate entities collided before resettling back into their own ghostly forms. Goosebumps danced along my skin and a chill ran up my spine. I was not ready for this. Ben, I could handle, but now I was a ghost whisperer?

"I know this is a lot to get your head around," I began, glancing toward the door, "but we don't have much time. I'm not meant to be here and the police won't be too happy with me if I get caught. Do you remember what happened?"

Myra shook her head. "The last thing I remember was arriving here, getting ready to open..." she squeezed her eyes shut. "Why can't I remember?"

"Ben was the same." I told her. "He couldn't remember anything about his death nor the events immediately leading up to it. Or anything about the cases he'd been working on." I shot Ben an accusatory glance. I'd have been able to solve his murder a whole lot faster if he'd been able to remember what had happened.

"Cases?"

"Ben was a PI too. It's his business that I've taken over." I explained. "I really can't explain why you can't remember. Some sort of amnesia thing when you crossed over, I guess." I stood up and began walking around her store. While Ashley's shop next door had been airy and light, Myra's was dark and moody. She had similar things on her shelves, candles and incense, tarot cards and books on how to use them. A lovely collection of silver chalices caught my eye. "Do you practice witchcraft?" I asked, a flash of Mrs. Hill appearing in my mind. She had similar items on her altar.

"No." Myra sounded affronted. "I'm a psychic not a witch."

My mouth turned down at the corners. I couldn't see much of a distinction, figured I'd look into it later, do some research between the two. Maybe that would explain why I now had two ghostly companions. Both Ben and Myra had connections with the occult, no matter how tenuous. "Did you have an appointment book or diary?"

Myra rose, and I got my first really good look at her. She was tall and slim and stunning. Her ebony hair was piled half up and half down, captured beneath the scarf. Around her neck were multiple necklaces, and like Ashley next door, she had multiple bracelets on her wrists. Myra also sported rings on every finger, some containing gemstones, some not. Her purple and black boho blouse was loose and flowy, in stark contrast to the skintight black leather pants and three inch ankle boots. I remembered Ashley had told me she was thirty-three, but in all honesty Myra Hansen didn't look a day over twenty-five. Now that the crying had stopped, and the blotchiness was leaving her face, I could see she had impeccably applied black eyeliner that winged up into a classic cat eye effect. And a dark purple lipstick that was two shades off being black. She breezed past me, to a velvet curtain hanging at the rear of the shop, and disappeared through it. I followed. It was a tiny office, about the size of my bathroom. Cardboard boxes were stacked on one side, reaching nearly to the ceiling. There was a tiny desk, more of a hallway table than an actual desk. Myra stood in front of it.

"It should be here." She said, pointing to the surface of the table that was littered with paper, pens and business cards.

"The police probably took it." Ben said, poking his head through the wall.

"I do remember something," Myra said, "my first client was Jacob, but he wasn't due until ten."

"You remember that?" I was surprised. Ben had remembered nothing remotely useful from the time surrounding his death. She nodded. "I always open at nine. Always. I get a lot of walk-ins for either tarot readings or palm reading. My regulars book a time so they're not held up waiting for me."

"And business was good? How many regulars are we talking about?"

Myra counted off on her fingers. "Jacob Henry has been visiting me frequently for a few weeks now. He comes in almost daily. Then we have Mrs. Davis. Regina Davis. She comes in once a week. And then there's Kit Chambers, she comes in, oooh, maybe once a month. Sometimes every second week if she has something happening in her life that she particularly wants guidance on."

"You said Jacob had an appointment today. What about Regina, when did you last see her?"

"Regina comes in every Wednesday at nine thirty. It's the same time she used to take her poodle, Rufus, to the groomers. She felt closer to him at those times, so we set it up as an ongoing thing."

"Were you really channeling a dead dog? Or were

you just taking Regina's money and telling her what she wanted to hear?"

The look Myra shot me made me shiver. "Easy there, cowboy." Ben drawled near my ear, "she's the victim here, not a suspect."

"It could be relevant." I huffed, "what if Regina figured out Myra was taking her for a ride and killed her in a fit of rage, devastated that she hadn't been communicating with Rufus?"

Myra snorted, interrupting us. "You're either a believer or a non-believer," she eyeballed me up and down, reminding me I was still in yesterday's clothes after sleeping over at Ben's house. "But considering you're having this discussion with two dead people..." her raised brow spoke volumes. Fair point.

"Okay," I cleared my throat. "You mentioned a third client. Kit Chambers?"

Myra chewed on her lip and studied the ceiling. "It's hard to say for sure without my appointment book... but it wasn't in the last two weeks. Kit is on vacation back home."

"Where's that?"

"England. Essex, if I remember correctly."

"Oh, so she's British?" My thoughts swung to Thor and his adorable British accent.

"She is. She's a web developer, travels all around

the world. Has been here for … oh, it has to be over three months now."

"But you said she's on vacation? Is she coming back to Firefly Bay? Or is she just moving on, greener pastures and all that?"

Myra shrugged. "All I know is what she told me. That's she's going on vacation and she'll see me when she gets back. She said she'd be gone about a month, something about her grandmother's estate and family commitments—although her family drove her to travel in the first place."

I pulled out my phone to make a note of everything she'd just told me but the empty black screen staring up at me was a jarring reminder that the battery was flat and I didn't have my charger. I made yet another mental note to buy one of those portable charger packs. Eyeing the contents of the small desk, I grabbed a pen and business card and wrote the three names of Myra's regular clients on the back.

"And that's it for regular clients? Everyone else was a one-off? Do any of them stand out? Anyone have a reaction to a reading? Unhappy or angry?"

Myra tossed a few loose strands of hair over one shoulder and propped a hand on her hip. "My clients always leave satisfied." With her nose in the air she swiveled and, well if a ghost could stride, that's what I imagined she was doing, back into her store. She came to a halt by the round table draped in the black tablecloth, her workstation for want of a better word, and peered at the floor in utter concentration. Curious, I joined her. Ahhh. There was a small puddle of blood. I hadn't noticed it when I came in, it blended so well with the dark rug beneath the table, but now I was closer I could smell the familiar coppery tang. I backed up. I hadn't thought to ask how Myra had died, but the blood told me it was a violent death. Like Ben's. Is that why they were both ghosts?

I glanced at Ben who was drifting around the store perusing the shelves. "Anything?" I asked. He turned and pointed to the table. "There's something under the table."

"What is it?" The tablecloth reached the floor, and I gingerly pinched the fabric between two fingers and lifted. I'd always imagined a psychic hid all their tricks under the tablecloth and now I was about to find out for sure. Color me surprised when there were no secret switches or buttons. Nor could I see anything on the floor, but if it was dark in the store, it was super dark beneath the table. "Are you sure?"

"Positive. I can't make it out, but it's there."

"It's not the murder weapon, is it?" I couldn't believe the cops hadn't searched under the table.

"Just get down on your hands and knees, Fitz, and feel around." Ben ordered. Grumbling to myself about bossy ghosts, I did as instructed, my hands feeling over the surface of the floor until they slid over something smooth. "Got it." I sat back on my haunches and held up a tarot card. It was the death card.

9

"What are you doing here?" Officer Mills screwed up his face as if he'd caught a whiff of something unpleasant. I returned the favor, wrinkling my nose as I looked him up and down. He didn't scare me, nor intimidate me. I disliked him, pure and simple.

"I'm here to see Detective Galloway." I didn't want to be here. I would have called if I could, but my phone was still dead despite searching Myra's shop for a charger and saving me from an unpleasant trip into the Firefly Bay Police Department. Even standing in the foyer had the hairs on my arms standing on end and my gut churning.

"What's it regarding?"

Damn. A legitimate question. One I baulked at answering. I ground my teeth, fishing around for a feasible excuse when who should walk through the door but Captain Cowboy Hot Pants himself. Oh, he was a sight to behold, dark denim jeans clinging in all the right places, broad shoulders encased by a snug black T-shirt with a checkered button down tossed over the top. As I drank him in, I wondered if he owned any other clothes, for I usually saw him in this ensemble. Well, not this one exactly, just replicas of it. Not that I was complaining, oh no, he wore this look well and the welcoming grin on his face set my heart to a rather rapid pitter patter in my chest.

"Audrey, glad you made it." He shot Mills an unreadable look as he approached and settled a hand against my lower back, guiding me toward his office. The heat of his touch burned—in a good way. "Come on through." I let him lead me, for once lost for words.

In his office I sank into the chair opposite his desk, watched as he lowered his big frame into his own chair and leant back, elbows resting on the armrests, hands clasped loosely across his stomach, face expectant. Neither of us spoke and as the seconds ticked by I squirmed in my seat until he grinned, flashing a dimple. "Relax," he drawled. "It's just me. And I'm one of the good guys."

I frowned that he knew me so well, that he knew how uneasy I was being here, in the lion's den. My anxiety over the whole situation of corrupt police shot up a notch. I couldn't be here, I couldn't do this. Working with the police? Co-operating? Was I insane? This would not end well and I feared it would be me who'd come out the other side battered and broken. I glanced around, searching for Ben, needing his reassurance that I was doing the right thing, that I could trust Galloway, for despite my intense, scorch your panties off attraction to him, he was still a cop, and embedded in my psyche was cops were bad.

But Ben was annoyingly absent. As soon as I'd pulled up out front he'd shot inside and I figured he was having a good old sticky beak at his old workplace. I just hoped he'd stumble across something relevant to our case so I could solve Myra's murder and she could cross over. I'd been concerned how on earth I would wrangle two ghosts without being shown to my own bed in the psych ward, but I needn't have worried. It was the oddest thing. When Myra had tried to leave her store? She couldn't. It seemed Myra was confined to Nether &

Void. I had no answers why and had no-one to ask. Thinking of Myra did the trick, though. My heart rate slowed, my tension eased. I was working a case; I reminded myself, and despite everything else going on, I had a job to do.

"Couple of things." I said, my voice coming out like rusty nails. I cleared my throat and tried again. "Couple of things. First, do you have a charger?" I held up my phone. "Batteries dead." Our fingers brushed when he took the phone from me, and obliging plugged it into his charger.

"And the other thing?"

Reaching into my back pocket, I pulled out the Tarot card I'd found under Myra's table, careful to hold it by its corner to minimize fingerprints. "Your guys missed this. From Myra Hansen's crime scene."

Leaning forward, he took the card from me, mimicking my hold. "What—exactly—were you doing at Myra's?" he asked. His tone was conversational, but I'd seen the flash in his eyes, half worry, half suspicion.

"Ashley Baker hired me to find out who killed Myra. I was working the case." It came out like a defiant teenager who had just one upped her parents. Defensive, but with the certain smugness that she was right.

"And you're here to discuss this with me as your supervisor, right? Considering you just totaled your car because you were being chased by gunmen who may or may not have been involved in a bank robbery. That you were also involved in."

"Well, that too." It was my turn to lean forward, "Look, like it or not, I'm on the case. I'm here," I shot an uncomfortable look at the closed door, "when I really don't want to be."

He studied me intently for several heartbeats, his eyes not missing a thing, from my rapid breathing to the sweat beading my brow. "What has you so worked up about being here?"

I dropped my voice. "Have you checked your office for bugs?"

He jerked back, surprised. "You think I need to?"

I was about to tell him that yes; I did think he needed to, given he was apparently investigating corruption under this very roof when he held up his hand to silence me. "Point taken." His voice rolled out, deep and low, a rumble that vibrated through me. His gray eyes had darkened like an approaching storm and I wondered what had triggered his response. He blinked, his eyes lightened, and I watched as he slid the Tarot card into an evidence bag, unplugged my phone and handed it back to me, and stood. "Let's take this someplace else. I could use a decent coffee."

Ahhh. Good to see we were finally on the same page. I wasn't convinced these walls didn't have ears, and it seemed Galloway was in agreement. I shot a quick look around the room to see if Ben had returned. Nope. Too bad, he'd just have to catch up with us later.

Out in the parking lot I stood by my sturdy backup, my seventies era Chrysler, who'd been in retirement in Ben's garage but was now back on duty. "I'll meet you at Ben's place. I have decent coffee." I said, resting my hand on the roof.

"Ben's place? Don't you mean your place?"

"Semantics." Flipping him a grin, I slid into the driver's seat and slammed the door. It didn't catch, so I slammed it again. Third time was the charm. I patted the dash in gratitude when the engine started first try, albeit with a loud backfire and a cloud of smoke. Pulling out of the lot, I kept my eyes on the road and not a certain SUV that tailed me all the way to Ben's house.

"Oh good, you're back, I'm starving!" Thor greeted me at the door, and I bent down to scratch his head. "You're always starving." I told him, leaving the front door open for Galloway. In the kitchen, I left my phone on the counter. The slight amount of juice Galloway had given it wasn't enough to even turn it on.

"Excuse me!" Thor demanded, sitting in front of his bowl. I checked. Yep, still had kibble. Rearranging the biscuits in his bowl into a neat little pile, I stood back and watched the giant teddy bear of a cat nod his head in apparent satisfaction and begin crunching the kibble.

Just like he had many times before, Galloway took charge of the coffee machine and I slid onto a kitchen stool and watched him. It wasn't a hardship. He plugged something into the spare power socket, then grabbed my phone and plugged it in, all without a word. I figured he must've had a spare charger in his car.

He spoke with his back to me. "Tell me what you got." He commanded.

"What I've got?" I frowned.

"Your case." He prompted, and I blushed. For a moment, with the distraction of Captain Cowboy Hot Pants moving about in front of me, I'd forgotten all about the case and Myra.

Clearing my throat, I began. "Ashley Baker owns the new age shop next door to Myra, Nine. She hired me this morning."

"She rang you?"

"What? No. Lemme take a step back. I caught the news this morning, I was watching the story on the bank robbery," I couldn't contain a grin. "I got some press out of that. Anyway, the next story was Myra's murder, and I saw Jacob Henry, the clerk from the bank, and it seemed bizarrely coincidental, so I went down there. You lot had already left. Ashley recognized me and hired me on the spot."

"And your next course of action was to break into Myra's shop?" Galloway prompted. I snorted. "No. I didn't break into anything. I had a key."

I didn't miss the rolled eyes, but thankfully he didn't call me out on it. It was a crime scene, and I had ignored the tape across the door telling me to keep my ass out.

Galloway slid a steaming mug toward me. "You look good by the way."

I blinked in shock. "Errrr. Thanks?" One minute we'd been talking about Myra's murder and suddenly he tells me I look good? I mean, I'll take it, but...

He chuckled. "What I mean is you've pulled up okay after the accident. I admit I was surprised to see you in the station, I was expecting you to be laid up in bed for a few days."

"Yes, well, a massage by Ashley with her special oils helped a lot with that." Ashley's treatment had worked wonders. I was still sore and my muscles still twinged, but it was bearable.

Galloway seated himself on the stool next to me and waved a hand. "Continue. You let yourself into the crime scene. Then what?"

"Not much. At first I didn't even see the blood, couldn't smell it over the incense, but yeah, underneath her chair, a small pool of blood had soaked into the rug, so I'm assuming she was stabbed or shot." Galloway said nothing, so I continued. "I couldn't find her appointment book so I guess the police have it, but I did get some information from Ashley on who Myra's regulars were." I ticked off on my fingers. "Jacob Henry saw Myra frequently. And I mean frequently. Pretty much daily. Regina Davis saw her on a weekly basis, and Kit Chambers saw her semi-regularly, but Kit is on vacation back in England."

"Those are your suspects?"

"There's also a boyfriend. Lee. He's quite a bit older than Myra."

"And that makes him a suspect?"

"Pft. No. It was just an observation." I took a sip of my coffee, scalding my tongue. "I found the Tarot card under the table. To be fair, I didn't see it, I felt it, but if your officers had been using their flashlights, there's no excuse for them not to have found it."

Galloway ignored my dig. "Odd that it was under the table." He said, cradling his own coffee cup inches from his lips. "What were you doing under there?"

"Looking for tricks. Hidden switches and the like." It was a half truth. "But I've been thinking about the card. If she'd dropped it, it would have been in plain sight, on the floor. Not under the table."

"What does that tell you?"

Oh, good. A quiz. "That there was a struggle?" I chewed my lip, imaging the scene in my mind. "Myra had opened the store and was preparing for her first client of the day. She'd told me she opened at nine, but Jacob wasn't due until ten, so she had time for a walk-in or two before he arrived. What would you do while waiting for customers? Shuffle the Tarot. Maybe do a reading on yourself. Her killer arrives. Seats himself opposite her and she deals the cards. Places the deck on the table. Then things go pear-shaped. The customer doesn't like the reading. Or maybe he thinks it's all BS. Maybe he intentionally sweeps the cards off the table in anger.

Or flips the table. Then kills Myra." I paused, thinking. "She's dead and he... takes the time to straighten up, to put the cards back on the table, only he misses one."

I glanced up to see Galloway looking at me. "She told you?"

Crap! I'd slipped. It had been Myra who'd given me the information, but considering she was a ghost, I couldn't tell him that. My hands flailed around in panic. "Ashley." I pounced on the only name I could think of. "Ashley told me Myra opened at nine and that she took her first bookings from ten to allow for walk-ins."

Galloway nodded, that dimple flashing again. "Actually, that's not bad. Plausible. Only I'd change a couple of things."

I breathed a sigh of relief. He'd bought it. "Oh?"

"The killer didn't just tidy up the cards, he took them with him. There were no Tarot cards at the scene. Well, other than the ones Myra had for sale, that is. We didn't even realize they were missing, not until you turned up with that card."

"And the other thing?"

"She was stabbed in the back. Blade went straight into her heart."

I swallowed. At least it was quick. "That tells us

she knew her killer. It was someone she trusted, someone she was comfortable with, it didn't alarm her he was behind her." I said.

"Unless she didn't know they were there." Galloway pointed out. True. Maybe the killer had been hiding, waiting to strike, sneaking up behind her and taking her unaware.

"Was she sitting down? At her table?" That's how I'd found ghost Myra, sitting at her table with her head in her hands, screaming her lungs out. I figured that's where she'd died.

"She was. Why's that?"

"Because Myra was reasonably tall. If you wanted to stab her in the heart, you'd have to be a similar height."

"Or... wait until she was sitting down." Galloway pointed out.

"Which means... she wasn't killed in a fit of rage. Whoever did this? Planned it. It was premeditated." We had a cold-blooded killer in Firefly Bay. A shiver danced over my skin, raising goosebumps. My sixth sense was tingling, warning me none of this would end well. Galloway confirmed it when he turned to me and said, "you're not doing this one solo."

I blinked. "What?"

"This is dangerous, Audrey. And like it or not, you're still in training."

"I'm halfway through." I argued, but in all honesty, if he was offering to work the case with me, I wouldn't complain. The maniacs with the guns had rattled me. Was the bank robbery connected to Myra's death? Or was the fact that Jacob Henry had been present at both purely coincidental?

"You're with me on this one." His tone brooked no argument. With his stormy eyes so tantalizingly close, I did the first thing that popped into my head. I kissed him. A quick peck on the lips, but it was enough to ignite a fire in my belly. Galloway briefly rested his forehead against mine. "I'll take that as a yes."

10

*G*alloway hadn't been kidding when he said I was with him. Riding shotgun in his SUV we headed into town, first stop, the Firefly Bay Community Bank. It was a two birds scenario. I still hadn't signed the errant document that had triggered this whole series of events, and we needed to talk to Jacob Henry. Ben had caught up with us, materializing in the back seat, startling me so much I'd yelped and then had to brush Galloway off with a lame excuse about a cramp. I'm not sure he bought it, but he didn't call me on it, and for that I was grateful.

"Promise me you'll wait for me before you talk to Jacob." I demanded, stepping through the doors of the bank with Galloway behind me, radiating a lovely warm, comforting heat. In front of me, Ben, doing the exact opposite.

"I'll wait." I could hear the smile in his voice, didn't need to turn around to have it confirmed.

Susan caught sight of me and hurried from behind her service desk to envelope me in a bear hug. I tried not to wince as she squeezed my bruised shoulder. "Audrey, how are you?" She ran her hands up and down my upper arms, "all recovered?"

"Errr." I cast a quick glance at Galloway. Did people know about my car accident? Granted, word traveled fast in Firefly Bay, but I thought I'd managed to sneak this one under the wire. Galloway shrugged.

"From the bank robbery, silly." Susan chided, dragging me over to her workstation.

"Yes. I'm all... recovered... thank you. How about you?" So much had happened since then that the robbery felt far from a recent memory.

She typed something into her computer, then pulled open the drawer and retrieved a piece of paper. "I'm fine. I was rattled at the time, but the bank has offered counseling, which I took advantage of. Here, I still had this out and ready for you from yesterday."

Placing the document on the desk, she handed

me a pen, and I dutifully signed where she pointed. "All done now? That's it? You don't need anything else?"

She beamed at me, the smile one hundred percent fake, and I realized that Susan wasn't as okay as she said she was. Who would be after having masked gun wielding bandits storm into your place of work and here you were, a day later, standing in that exact same spot, pretending nothing ever happened? This time it was me who patted Susan's arm. "Thanks for everything, Susan. Take it easy, okay?"

Seeing our business was concluded, Galloway spoke up. "We'd like a word with Jacob Henry if he's around?"

"He's got today off. Compassionate leave since he found that psychic woman." Susan sniffed, her disapproval palpable.

"You're not a believer?" I guessed.

"Pft. It's a load of nonsense. But she had her hooks into Jacob, nice and deep. Spending all that money on some floozy who was supposedly helping him get his wife back when anyone can see that it ain't ever going to happen. That girl lost interest in him as soon as the wedding was over."

Galloway and I exchanged a look. "So you know his wife?" I asked.

"Of course. Don't get me wrong, I think it's a damn shame what she did to him, absolutely broke his heart she did. They'd been sweethearts for a while and... well I don't know. Maybe she was genuine, maybe not. All Jacob ever wanted was his own family, you know? The white picket fence, the kids, the wife, the whole thing. He was an only child and his mom a single parent and I think his childhood was lonely and he wanted more for himself. He thought he'd found it in Emily—we all did—but she's young, they both are, maybe she realized she was in over her head?"

"So they weren't married long?"

Susan was shaking her head, "Not even a year, coming up to their first anniversary in a couple of months."

"And that's what you think it was? That Emily was just in it for the wedding itself? One big party and then..."

"She was spoiled, that one." Susan leaned in. "Everything she ever wanted, her parents provided. So when she wanted a big fancy wedding, that's what she got. But then suddenly she wasn't under mummy and daddy's roof anymore, they weren't providing for her. Jacob was."

"And he didn't have the same financial resources I'm guessing." Galloway's voice was droll, like he'd heard it all before. In his line of work, he probably had.

"You got it. Oh, that poor naïve boy," she sighed, clutched a hand to her chest. "He was so clueless when it came to her. He was excited to be married, even more excited after the wedding, he was already talking about saving for a deposit on a house and then starting a family."

"And she wasn't on board with that?"

"Emily came from a comfortable upbringing." Susan shrugged. "Even though she knew she'd be living with Jacob in his apartment once they were married, I think the reality of it was a shock to her. And I don't know, maybe she was expecting mom and dad to buy them a house as a wedding present."

"They weren't living together before the wedding?" That surprised me. Most couples cohabitated before tying the knot these days.

Susan shook her head, "Nu-uh. Jacob was real traditional that way."

The bank doors slid open behind us and a customer

walked in, drawing Susan's attention away. "Oh, hi, Mrs. Green!" She waved and then glanced back at us. "Was there anything else I can help you with today?"

"No thanks, Susan. Take care." She'd relaxed a ton while gossiping about Jacob, but I'd seen the way she'd tensed when the doors opened, the way her eyes had darted toward the door, body rigid, before relaxing when she'd recognized Mrs. Green.

Ben, who'd disappeared through the back wall, returned. "Henry isn't here," he confirmed. I gave him the slightest of nods while following Galloway back to his SUV. "What next?" I asked, watching while he did something with his phone. Without looking up he said, "you tell me. It's your investigation."

"We go see Jacob at his home." I didn't even have to think about it. Jacob was in this up to his neck, I just needed to work out exactly what *this* was.

"Which is where?"

"Oh." Good point. I didn't have Jacob's address and hadn't thought to ask Susan for it. I'd have been surprised if she'd given it to me though, what with privacy laws and all that. Galloway flashed his phone at me. "Good thing I have his address, hmmm?"

"Oh ha ha," I joked. "You could have said."

"Nah, it's too much fun watching you think. Your

face is an open book." He started the car and headed us toward Jacob's apartment, which wasn't far from the bank, walking distance in fact.

"You will have to work on your poker face, Fitz." Ben teased, poking me in the shoulder. I ignored the icy blast. And my best friend.

"Do you think Jacob could have done it?" I asked, worrying my lip with my teeth. "Given that he was desperate to get his wife back and that Myra was apparently helping him? He must have spent a fortune visiting her. I wonder what she told him that kept him coming back?"

"He had opportunity. As to motive? We don't know how he felt about Myra, we can't go on gossip from a co-worker. He may have found her help invaluable. Or maybe he realized he was handing over his hard earned money for nothing. We won't know until we talk to him."

Fair point. We pulled up outside a three-story apartment building. I followed Galloway to the top floor—there was no elevator, which must be a pain if you lived here and had to lug groceries up three flights of stairs. Maybe that's why Emily left—if she was the poor little rich girl Susan painted her to be, living in such a place could have been a deal breaker. But then, she must have visited Jacob at his apartment, spent time here, so it shouldn't have come as a surprise.

Ben had gone on ahead, stuck his head back to talk to us when we'd arrived, only Galloway rang the bell and banged on the door, his knuckles going right through Ben's forehead. I cringed. For his part, Ben just grinned, but I saw Galloway frown and stare at his fingers, giving them a shake.

"No-one's home." Ben said, moving out of Galloway's way to stand by my side. "Did you do that on purpose?" I whispered out the corner of my mouth.

"What? Plant my face in the middle of Kade's fist? Why would I do that, Fitz?" I narrowed my eyes. I wasn't sure if Ben was teasing or not. I stood in the hallway, toeing the faded carpet, while Galloway gave the door another rap with his knuckles. Silence from inside. I could hardly tell Galloway that a ghost had told me no-one was home. We waited another couple of minutes, then returned to the car. "We'll circle back around to him." Galloway said, sliding behind the wheel and turning to face me, resting one arm on the steering wheel. "If necessary I can call in a welfare check."

"Welfare check?"

"If someone has concerns for his safety, that he

may be unwell or have self harmed, we can conduct a welfare—or wellness—check to make sure he's okay."

"So you'd bust his door in?"

Galloway snorted. "We'd ask the superintendent to unlock the door with his master key if we thought the situation warranted it."

"Do you think Jacob would do something like that?" My voice dropped, "that he'd... take his own life?"

"Relax, Fitz," Ben said from the back seat, "I already told you, Jacob Henry is not home. He's not swinging from the rafters or whatever other thing you're over active imagination is conjuring up."

"So far I've seen nothing to suggest that. Relax, we're not there yet, it's just an option for later if we can't track him down. He could be out getting some fresh air, buying a coffee, visiting a friend. So where to next, PI in training?" Galloway said. I ignored Ben and focused on Galloway.

Tipping my head back against the headrest, I gazed up at the roof of the car, mentally going through my list of suspects. "Regina Davis." I turned my head to look at Galloway, who nodded, already punching her name into his phone. "What do you have there, anyway?" I asked. "Some sort of app?"

"Something like that, yes. And before you ask, no, you can't have one too. Police issue only."

I pouted, it'd be nice to have access to the police database, it would make life easier.

---

*R*egina Davis lived in a mansion overlooking Firefly Bay. A maid ushered us inside, informing us that Mrs. Davis was taking cocktails by the pool. Galloway had raised his eyebrows and glanced at his watch. I agreed. Little early in the day for cocktails, never-the-less, we followed the maid out to the pool which was straight out of a five-star luxury resort. Sunlight glistened off the pool's surface, lounge chairs were scattered around the perimeter, but the view? Man, the view was to die for. Three hundred and sixty-five degrees of ocean and coastline. It was breathtaking.

"The police are here to see you." The maid announced, then swiveled on her heel and quickly disappeared. Regina was sitting at a table beneath an umbrella with her laptop open in front of her, a tall glass of something in front of her. She stood as we approached, looking cool, calm, and classy in her white pants and leopard print blouse, gold hoops in her ears, a matching gold chain around her neck and wrist, and Prada sunglasses.

"Please," she smiled, her red lipstick brilliant in the sunlight, "take a seat. Can I offer you a drink?"

"Bit early in the day, isn't it?" I asked, nodding at her glass. She laughed. "Darling, it's past midday, but relax, it's a mocktail. You want one? I can get Louise to whip up anything you want."

I shook my head. "I'm good." I settled into a chair opposite her, Galloway took the one to my left. Ben did what he usually did, disappeared to check out the rest of the house.

Regina eyed us up and down. "To what do I owe the pleasure?"

"I'm Detective Kade Galloway. This is my associate, Audrey Fitzgerald." Galloway introduced us, producing a business card from his pocket and sliding it across the table where Regina glanced at it without picking it up. "We're here about Myra Hansen."

Regina's hand went to her throat, and beneath her heavy layer of makeup, she paled. "I heard! How awful."

"We believe you were a client of Myra's?" Galloway prompted.

Regina nodded, reaching for her glass with a

trembling hand she took a hefty sip. Bet she was wishing it wasn't a mocktail now, the look on her face telling me a double shot of vodka would be welcome. She cleared her throat. "Yes, I saw Myra every week, we had an ongoing arrangement."

Galloway nodded. We already knew that. I wondered if she would fess up that the reason she was seeing a psychic was to communicate with her dead dog. Color me surprised when those were the very next words out of her mouth. "People think I'm crazy, but you know what? I really don't care. I went to Myra so I could check on Rufus, my poodle, check that he was okay, that he was happy on the other side, and just to feel closer to him. I know, I know, he was a dog, but to me he was more, I loved him, we were soul mates." She sat back, head moving from me to Galloway and back again, eyes hidden by the dark shades.

"Soul mates?" I couldn't help myself. I was intrigued.

Regina's lips curled into a sad smile. "Sounds crazy, right? But you think having all of this," she waved her hand around, indicating the luxurious house and gardens, "can make you happy? Think again. You can be the richest of the rich and still be lonely."

"Are you? Lonely?"

She chuckled. "No, not really. I was born into this life, I've never known anything different. Everyone thinks it's Robert who has the money and I'm happy enough for them to think that, but the truth is, he's the one who had to sign the pre-nup."

"Robert's your husband?" Galloway asked. She nodded. "Married for twenty years. No kids. Robert bought me Rufus as a wedding anniversary present. That's when I discovered Rufus was the one who fulfilled me, who filled a space in my heart that I didn't know needed filling. We were inseparable until he passed away."

"And your husband was never jealous over your relationship with your dog?" Oh God, I felt stupid for even saying it, but the way Regina gushed over her pooch, I figured it was a legitimate question.

"Robert is too busy schtupping his secretary to be bothered one way or the other about me."

Galloway and I glanced at each other. He motioned for me to close my mouth. I did. With a snap.

"You're saying your husband is having an affair with his secretary?" Galloway needed confirmation. Regina happily gave it. "Oh, yes. It's been going on for years."

"And you're not... upset?" I was beyond shocked. If my husband had been cheating on me—for years —I'd have his gonads as souvenirs on my desk. That's if I had a husband. Which I don't, but the sentiment is still the same.

"Darling, why would I be? The man is doing me a favor. Robert has needs—as do I—but let's just say neither of us is best suited to fulfilling those needs."

Oooh, I could feel my mouth getting ready to drop open again so I clamped my teeth together, hard. Robert's secretary was a man. Robert was gay. Or at least bi.

"Where were you this morning between nine and nine-thirty?" Galloway brought conversation back on track while my mind was still grappling with the fact that Regina's husband was having an affair with his male secretary and she was perfectly okay with it. Or did it just seem that way?

Regina leaned forward and tapped a key on her laptop, I assumed to bring up her diary, which struck me as odd since we were only asking her movements from a handful of hours ago. I wouldn't have thought it was that hard to remember. "I had a personal training session." She told us.

"With?"

"Jayden Ellis. You can ask him, he'll confirm."

Then, to my utter surprise, her chin wobbled. *Was she? Crying?* A tear escaped from beneath the Prada shades and trickled down her cheek. She quickly wiped it away.

"Are you okay?" I asked. I hadn't realized she was so close to Myra, but I guess if they'd been having regular sessions, maybe they'd developed a friendship of sorts.

"I don't know what I'm going to do." She sniffed, "how am I going to talk to Rufus now?" She leaned forward and began typing into the laptop. "There have to be other psychics around!"

Right. Not tears for the dead psychic. Tears because she'd lost the connection to her pet. Galloway stood, and I followed suit.

"Thanks for talking with us, we'll be back if we have any further questions. If you think of anything, anything at all that might help in our investigation, please give me a call." He said, tapping the business card on the table. Darn. I still didn't have business cards. I made yet another mental note to get some organized.

"Sure, sure." She didn't even look up, intent on her google search for psychics, I presumed. We let ourselves out. I wasn't convinced Regina Davis was our murderer. Messed up, hell yes, but not a killer.

11

"*M*an, you should have seen that house, Fitz!" Ben gushed, leaning forward from the back seat and talking straight into my ear. "It was HUGE! Oh, and get this, there's a locked door in the basement!"

I swiveled to look at him. "A locked door?"

"You will never guess what's inside." He crossed his arms and flopped back against the seat, a smug expression on his face.

"Okay, you're right, I'm not going to guess. What was behind the locked door?"

Shooting forward again, his voice dropped. "A red room."

I frowned. "A red room?"

He nodded. "A red room."

"As in... fifty shades?" I blinked, my mind grappling to come to terms that someone legitimately had a room full of sex toys and equipment.

"Uh-huh."

"I wonder who uses it. Her or him?"

"Want me to come back and find out?" Ben offered.

"So kind of you to offer so selflessly," I drawled, "but that won't be necessary. Perv." I added.

The driver's side door opened, and Galloway slid behind the wheel. "Who are you talking to?"

I flattened my lips into a straight line. It was a legitimate question, and I was so busted. "Myself?" He can't have missed the fact that I'd been having a conversation with his rear seat, but I lived in hope.

Firing up the engine, Galloway shot me a look. A look that he said he didn't believe me. At all. "Sure." That one word was laced with derision.

"You're so busted." Ben said helpfully. I almost told him to shut up. Almost. While my mind was scrambling for a way out, I was saved by the bell. My phone started buzzing.

"Hey, mom." I'd never been so grateful for a call from my mom in my entire life.

"Hey, sweetheart, just checking in, you still okay for dinner this week?"

"Sure, mom. Wouldn't miss it." Our weekly family get-togethers were a tradition, I figured it wasn't the reason for her call. "What's up, mom?"

"Well," she paused, "your father and I saw you on the news..."

Oh. The bank robbery. "I'm fine, mom, honestly. It was scary at the time, but no-one got hurt." I kicked myself for not thinking to ring her after my face was plastered on the news—it wouldn't have been very nice to find out your daughter had been involved in a bank heist from a TV reporter. "I'm sorry I didn't call."

"You know we worry about you." She sniffed. Correction. Mom worried. Dad just supported mom in her concern. But if he knew I'd totaled Ben's car escaping from bad guys wielding guns, well then yes, I'd say his worry would far outstrip my moms. Which is why I had no intention of telling them. Ever. "Look mom, I'm working at the moment, I have a case, but I'll see you for dinner on Friday and I'll tell you all about it then, I promise."

"Okay, love. Just... be careful. Love you."

"Love you too, mom." Sliding my phone back into

my bag I glanced at Galloway out the corner of my eye. "That was mom," I said.

"Yeah, I got that." Of course he did. I wanted to smack my forehead with the palm of my hand but stopped the impulse by sitting on my hands instead. We traveled in silence for a few minutes until I realized we were heading back to the station. My shoulders slumped. I'd been enjoying working with him, but I figured he had work he had to do that didn't involve dragging a novice PI around. Especially one who held full-on conversations with herself. "Heading back, huh?"

"Oh, yeah, sorry—I got a message I'm needed back at the station. We will have to cut this short."

"Oh. Okay." I thought I did a good job of hiding my disappointment, I even managed to ignore Ben, who'd started chatting again in the back. "I don't think Regina Davis is our man," he said. "I can guarantee you Kade will check her alibi, make sure she was at a training session with Ellis. But," he paused to drag in a breath, which was curious since ghosts can't—or don't need to—breathe. "That's not to say she didn't hire someone to do her dirty work. She has the money. Our hypothesis still rings true. If she discovered Myra was a fraud would she lash out in such a way? Extreme yes. But effective. And she said it herself, she grew up with money, in a world where money solves all your problems, one way or another."

He had a point. Regina had money. But from what she told us, she was lacking in motive. One thing I learned in PI school? *Everyone lies.* So what was Regina Davis lying about? The status quo in her marriage? Her finances? Or the whole visiting a psychic to talk to her dead dog thing? My gut was telling me that Regina didn't kill Myra, but with nothing to back that up...

"Sorry to cut this short." We'd pulled into the parking lot without me even noticing. "I'll swing by later and pick you up to go visit Jacob Henry."

The smile I sent him was nothing short of dazzling, I'm sure. He blinked, and that dimple appeared. "What? You thought I was ditching you? Audrey, you'd know if I were ditching you 'cos I'd literally tell you 'Audrey, I'm ditching you.' I legitimately have to come in; a meeting with the Chief that wasn't in my calendar." The last was said with a frown.

"Trouble?" I asked. In my experience, any meeting with the boss was a precursor to me getting fired. But then Galloway did not have the clumsy gene. He was solid, in more ways than one. I hitched a breath in shock. The thought he was solid, dependable, could be trusted, hit me in the center of my chest. Hard.

"Doubtful." He was halfway out the car and I was still sitting here, shocked at my own revelation. Hurriedly I unsnapped the seatbelt and opened the door, climbing out, only to have my leg snag on the lip of the footwell on the way out. "Argh!" I toppled, one leg caught in the car, the other landing painfully on my knee, my bag flinging over my head to land on the ground in front of me, contents spilling across the paved parking lot.

"Audrey?" Galloway rounded the rear of the car, caught an eyeful of me in a rather inelegant position, and promptly burst out laughing. "You okay?" He asked, stepping closer.

"I'm fine." I huffed, rolling onto my backside and extracting my foot from where it was caught. Climbing to my feet, I dusted myself off, ignoring the stinging in my knee—what was another bruise to add to the collection, anyway? Galloway joined me in picking up the contents of my bag and we were there, crouched close together, heads almost touching when it hit me. An urge to kiss him. Being this close, his scent all around me, playing on my senses and making me totally forget that I had a ghost as a chaperone.

"Audrey and Kade, sitting in a tree..." Ben sing-songed. But even Ben being a dick wasn't enough to dull the heat burning through my veins. My hand brushed his where we both dropped items into my bag at the same time. Me, a tube of lip balm. Him, a pack of tampons. I felt the heat creep up my face yet when I looked up and his eyes were on me, so close I could see the golden flecks in the otherwise sea of turbulent gray, I was lost. Dropping the balm, I reached up and laid my palm against his cheek. "Kade." I was so used to calling him Galloway that using his first name felt both foreign on my tongue and strangely right at home.

"Yeah?" The drawl was low, rumbling through me in a vibration to my very core. It was amazing I hadn't lost my balance yet, crouched as I was on the ground, and toppled right into him.

"You know that time when we kissed, and you said to let you know when I was ready?"

"Yeah?" His eyes darkened and yet he didn't move, letting me come to him like he'd promised he would. In my head I planned to go slow. In reality, I lurched forward and plastered my lips against his. We began to topple, but he flung out a hand to brace us against the side of his car. With the other, he held the nape of my neck and steadied me while I kissed him. Boy, did I kiss him. I kissed him until my lips tingled and my body was mush, I was liquid against him. Ignoring Ben, who was hooting and carrying on, I gave all of myself in that kiss. Of course I did. We were in the parking lot of the Firefly Bay Police Department and he was about to go into a meeting with the Chief. Perfect timing, perfect location.

Slowly we pulled away, breath mingling. "Right back at ya." His words resonated through my bones and my lips curled into a self-satisfied smile. I could have stayed in our little bubble of lust forever, but the front doors of the station opened and voices reached us. With a wry grin Galloway released me and stood, helping me to my feet. "I'll call you." He dropped a kiss on my cheek, swiveled on his heel and walked away. I watched until he disappeared inside, because watching that denim clad rear walk away was a sight I'd never tire of.

"When you've finished ogling," Ben drawled, "we should go. We've got work to do."

"Right!" Tugging on the hem of my T-shirt, I pulled myself together and headed toward my Chrysler, tossing my bag onto the passenger seat.

Ben seated himself on top of it. "Seriously?" I asked. "You couldn't just—"

"What? Sit in the back seat because your bag is here?" He cut in, his incredulous response told me what he thought of that idea. "Since when do you cart your handbag around with you, anyway?" He muttered, trying to push my bag to the floor with no success.

"Since now." Thankfully, my car started on the first try and I pulled out. It couldn't have been more than thirty seconds later when red and blue flashing lights lit up my rearview mirror. "What the hell?" Flipping on my indicator, I pulled over, watching as the patrol car followed.

"It's Mills." Ben said ominously. Winding down my window, I waited for Mills to reach me. "Something wrong, Officer?"

"License and registration."

Flipping open the glove compartment, I handed them over, watched while Mills glanced at them, then handed them back.

"Going to have to write you up for talking on your cell while driving." He drawled, one hand resting on his gun.

"What? I wasn't talking on my phone." I protested.

"I know what I saw."

"Uh, no you don't." I argued. "If I was talking on my phone, where is it?" I waved a hand in front of me, indicating my dash and empty cup holders where I normally stashed my phone when driving.

"You could have put it away when you saw me."

"But I didn't." This was bull hockey, and we both knew it.

"I'm going to have to ask you to step out of the vehicle ma'am."

"What! Why?" I protested. This was ridiculous.

"Do what he says, Audrey." Ben warned. "He's using his power against you and if you resist? Well, let's not give him a reason to shoot you, eh?" He was right. Mills' hand was resting on his revolver, fingers curled around the grip as if he'd like nothing more than to whip that bad boy out and put a bullet in me.

"Out of the car!" Mills suddenly shouted, "now!"

"Okay, okay," I opened the door and climbed out. Mills stepped forward, hand still on his gun, but he hadn't drawn it, and for that I was grateful. "Turn around, hands on the roof." I obeyed, although it killed me to do so. "Spread your legs." A booted foot kicked my ankle to hurry me along. The pat down that followed lasted way too long, with Mills pudgy fingers lingering in places they had no business lingering. I felt the heat in my cheeks but bit my tongue. I knew what he was doing, humiliating me like this. Ben was right, it was all a power play but despite everything, Mills was a police officer and I was a civilian and I had to obey his instructions. This was no routine traffic stop. This was harassment, pure and simple.

*A*fter my encounter with Mills, I was one hundred dollars poorer and one hundred percent pissed off. Ben told me I could appeal the charge, but really? What was the point, who would believe me over an officer of the law? This was the shit Ben had to deal with when he'd been a police officer, and my anger and frustration at his situation returned tenfold. Rather than return to Ben's, I swung back around to Jacob Henry's apartment. I needed to keep my mind off Officer Ian Mills and his bogus charge.

Ben saved me a trip up three flights of stairs by shooting ahead and doing a reconnaissance mission. "Nope still not home." He informed me on his return.

"Darn it." I tapped the steering wheel. "I wonder where he is?" The rumbling of my stomach interrupted my thought processes, and Ben's guffaw confirmed just how loud the rumble was. "Whoa, Fitz," he laughed, "better feed the beast."

Figuring food would probably help to appease my foul mood, I decided lunch at the Seaview Cafe was in order. Plus, I had an ulterior motive. Ben could go check in with Myra while I ate. Two birds, one stone. Ben was happy to oblige, and I figured he enjoyed having a ghostly pal—I was hoping between the two of them they could come up with an explanation why Myra can't leave the store. Not that it was important, I was merely curious. I waited until he'd disappeared through the front door of Nether & Void before making my way toward the cafe a few doors down. Standing inside, I paused while my eyes adjusted to the dim lighting, then glanced around. The place was bigger than I thought, with over two dozen tables scattered throughout. It was lunchtime, and the place was busy, almost every table occupied, when I spotted a familiar face.

"Hey, Audrey!" Ashley Baker stood and waved me over. "Come join us, there's room at our table."

I waved back and began weaving my way through

the tables while checking out Ashley's dining companion. He was an older guy with sunglasses perched atop his bald head, gray mustache, solid build. He was wearing a black leather jacket, and I wondered if he wasn't hot since it was a balmy eighty degrees out.

"Audrey, this is Lee Noble, Myra's boyfriend. Lee, this is the PI I hired, Audrey Fitzgerald," Ashley said. Lee stood and shook my hand, his massive paw crushing mine in a powerful grip. Across his knuckles, faded black tattoos. A diamond, club, heart, and spade. I figured Lee Noble was into gambling. Why else would you have a card deck tattooed on your fingers?

"Pleased to meet ya." His smile was polite and entirely fake. I matched it with one of my own, while surreptitiously flexing my bruised hand behind my back.

"Hi. Thanks for letting me join you. I had no idea this place was so busy." I slid into the seat next to Ashley. She nodded. "Yep, this place is always pumping at lunchtime." Her smile dimmed. "Myra and I used to like to people watch, make up stories about them to entertain ourselves."

Which reminded me. "I'm sorry for your loss." I said to Lee. He rolled one shoulder, the leather creaking. "Thanks." I waited for more, but it appeared Lee would not be forthcoming.

"So." I picked up the menu, knocking over the salt shaker in the process. "You two met through Myra?"

"Actually," Ashley said, leaning forward and righting the shaker, "I sort of already knew Lee. Knew of him anyway."

"Oh?" Hmmm. The club sandwich looked good. But then so did the burger. My stomach growled again, thankfully the noise of the cafe masked it.

"My sister's boyfriend." Ashley continued.

"Ash." Lee grumbled.

I glanced up at the warning in his voice, curious why he didn't want Ashley telling me about the connection between her sister's boyfriend and him. I made a mental note to check it out. Then frowned. I'd been making a lot of mental notes lately, I was going to need a Rolodex to keep them all organized.

"What?" Tossing her dreadlocks over one shoulder, she eyed him defiantly. "It's not a secret."

"You really want her knowing about Skye?"

I'd been about to ask who Skye was when a waitress appeared at our table. "You folks ready to order?" She asked, chewing gum. Crap, I hadn't decided yet, but considering how busy this place was, I'd better choose quickly. Who knows how long it would be before the waitress came back around again.

"I'll have the pear, pomegranate and roasted butternut squash salad with maple sesame vinaigrette." Ashley ordered. "And a green tea." The waitress swiped through the screen on her iPad and pressed a bunch of buttons, sending Ashley's order straight to the kitchen.

"And you, sir?" The waitress asked Lee. But Lee was shaking his head. He stood, straightening his jacket, and the waft of stale cigarette smoke and body odor had me wrinkling my nose in distaste. "Change of plans, Ash, sorry. Just remembered there's somewhere else I need to be." And with that, he walked away. Ashley watched him go with her mouth hanging open.

"Was it something I said?" I asked. Shaking herself out of her stupor, she turned to me. "Doubtful. He's shook up over Myra." I could tell she didn't entirely buy it, that his behavior was unusual, but also that she was covering for her rather rude friend.

"Do you want me to come back?" The waitress reminded us she was waiting to take my order. Absolutely not, I was starving. "I'll take the burger with extra fries, and a coke." I ordered.

After she'd gone I turned to Ashley, who was chewing a nail. "Sorry if I intruded." I got the distinct impression that Lee had left because of me, and I had to say I wasn't entirely sorry. He was what I'd call a bruiser. A big tough guy with tattoos on his knuckles and an overall demeanor that told me he solved his problems with his fists and not his voice.

"I know he doesn't look it, but inside, he's really hurting. Lee is one of those guys who doesn't wear his heart on his sleeve." She sighed, playing with the end of a dreadlock. "It's just so sad, you know? He'd been about to propose to Myra. She was all keyed up and excited, telling me things were finally going right and they had big plans. And while he is acting..." she cast her eyes to the ceiling as if the words she was searching for were printed there. "Distant. Like her death hasn't affected him that much, it really has. On the inside he's devastated that the love of his life, the woman he wanted to marry, has been violently murdered."

Interesting. I did not get that vibe from him at all. "He told you he was going to propose?"

She snorted. "No. We don't actually talk all that much. I just hear what Myra tells me."

"And she told you she thought he would propose?"

"Welllllll," Ashley hesitated. "Not exactly. I assumed. Because she was acting all excited and happy. She had this real energy about her."

And Ashley, being the romantic she is, assumed that because Myra was happy, it was because of Lee. I'd have to ask Myra about it myself, I'd drop in to the shop after lunch.

"You two have lunch together frequently?" I asked.

"No. Not at all."

"Oh! Then I really did scare him away." I joked. But it wasn't a joke, not really. Lee Noble had left because of me. Why? I wasn't law enforcement, but did he see me as a threat? And if so, why? Because he was guilty of his girlfriend's murder? "So how do you know him?" Time to find out more about the man who could potentially be a murderer. I was so glad I'd decided to have lunch here today.

"He knew my sister's boyfriend, Rhys." She fiddled with the salt shaker, spinning it around in her fingers. "I may as well tell you because you will probably find out anyway," she said, "my sister, Skye, is in jail for drug smuggling."

I blinked. Twice. I hadn't seen that coming, not at all. Pulling myself together, I placed my hand over

Ashley's to keep the salt shaker upright. "I'm sorry to hear that." I offered. "That can't be easy."

"She says she's innocent." Ashley's blue eyes turned glassy with unshed tears. "And I believe her."

"So... what? You think she was set up?"

"I think she was tricked." Ashley confirmed. "By Rhys. Her boyfriend."

"The same boyfriend who knows Lee?" My eyebrows shot into my hairline. Was Ashley accusing Lee of having links to organized crime? Because that's where my mind went.

She nodded. "Rhys Parker was the worst thing that ever happened to Skye."

"Tell me what happened." I leaned my chin on my hand and waited with bated breath.

"Rhys told her they'd won a vacation to Nassau, in the Bahamas. Seven days of sun, sand, and fun. Skye was so excited, she'd never traveled before and to go to the Caribbean was like a dream come true. But when they arrived, they searched her bags at customs and they found heroin hidden in the lining of her suitcase. It wasn't hers." Ashley quickly said. "Skye was a party girl, yes, but it was booze and maybe some marijuana, nothing heavier and she'd never sell drugs. Never."

"And you think Rhys hid the drugs in her bag?" I asked.

"Who else? He lied about winning the trip. He'd told her it was through some radio show, he'd been a lucky caller, but it turns out it was a total fabrication. That came out in court. But the magistrate was very..." she hesitated, searching for words. "He was like, the drugs were in her bags, she's responsible for her own bags, therefore she's responsible for the drugs. Full stop. Sentenced her to twenty years in jail."

"So Rhys got away, scot free?" I wish I could say it was a surprise, but it really wasn't. How many times did you hear on the news that someone had unwittingly been a drug mule? Someone they thought they could trust had hidden drugs in their belongings without their knowledge. But usually the courts knew that, could see the truth. Why then did Skye end up in jail if it was Rhys who was responsible? Was Skye another victim of a corrupt police force, bending the evidence to suit their own needs?

Ashley heaved a breath. "Yep. I don't know how he did it. The only fingerprints on Skye's suitcase were hers. They even found them inside the lining."

Oooooh. I studied Ashley intently. Her sister's

fingerprints were inside the lining of the suitcase, which was probably all the evidence the police needed to charge her.

"I hate to ask, but—" I paused, then blurted, "is there any way that Skye did this?"

"No!" Ashley was vehement. "Because none of her prints were on the drugs. The drugs were totally wiped clean. Why would you do that and not wipe down the inside of the case? But this is where it gets weird, because remember how I said that Rhys' prints weren't on the suitcase at all? Skye said he'd lifted her case into a cab and helped her with it at the airport. So he'd touched it. It should have had his prints on it."

"What do you think happened?"

"I think Rhys had lifted Skye's prints somehow and planted them inside the lining of the suitcase at the same time he stashed the drugs—all without her knowledge. But the one thing that's got me puzzled is how he wiped off his prints once they'd arrived at the airport. I mean, surely Skye would have noticed if he'd whipped out a rag and began wiping down the suitcase handle, right?"

"You'd think so, yes. So you suspect someone else was involved? Like a baggage handler? They'd have access."

Ashley was nodding, her head bopping up and down so fast her dreads flew. "Exactly. They wear gloves anyway, so a little vigorous attention to that particular suitcase handle would have removed all prints, then Skye grabbed it off the carousel at Nassau, so the only prints were hers."

Plausible. "And where does Lee come into all of this?"

"Well." She flipped her dreadlocks over her shoulder and leaned toward me. "Skye was still living in Portland. Oregon Portland, not Maine Portland—that's where I'm from, only I decided to get out. She stayed. Anyway, she met Rhys at a bar one night and they hooked up. Rhys was working at the docks at the time, and his supervisor was Lee Noble. I remember because it was Lee who picked Rhys up from the airport when he flew back from the Bahamas after the trial."

"How long ago was this?"

"Just over five years. I was living in Seattle at the time."

I drummed my fingers on the table, mind whirling. "Portland Oregon is a long way from Firefly Bay." I said, more to myself than to her. "Clear across the country."

"True. I slowly made my way from the West

Coast to East. Landed in Firefly Bay, oh, it'd be about two years ago now. I fell in love with the place and decided I'd set down some roots at long last."

"And you recognized Lee?" What were the chances that a man you'd seen in passing in Portland turned up in Firefly Bay?

But Ashley was shaking her head. "Not really. I only ever saw a picture of Lee on tv. I hadn't met him in real life. Not until he started dating Myra, and then only once or twice. I only figured out it was him when Myra told me in passing that he'd lived in Portland a few years ago. That's when I asked him if he knew Rhys. Since Lee works at the docks here, I assumed he'd worked at the docks in Portland, that maybe they'd crossed paths. He told me he'd been his supervisor, said he'd picked him up from the airport that day because his family didn't want the media scrutiny. He was doing him a favor, nothing more."

"And you believe that?" To be honest, I was skeptical.

Ashley laughed. "Once you get to know him, Lee is an absolute teddy bear. He looks like a thug, but on the inside he's a big softy. Only don't tell him I said that."

Our food arrived and as I sunk my teeth into my

burger, I pondered what Ashley had told me about Lee. Her view that he was a gentle giant did not ring true with the vibe I got from him, and I added yet another mental note to ask Galloway about not only Lee Noble, but Skye Baker's case.

*H*aving a ghost suddenly appear by your side in the middle of lunch was something I was not prepared for. "Bad news." Ben said, taking the seat Lee had vacated. I sucked in a startled breath and immediately choked on my mouthful of burger. Ben gave me a couple of hearty thumps on the back as I coughed until my eyes were streaming, but his hand passed right through me, freezing my lungs, which didn't help at all.

"Oh, my!" Ashley grabbed my arm, concerned. "Are you okay?"

"Urghhh." I choked, finally catching my breath. With a shaky hand, I reached for my coke and took a sip, the bubbles burning. "Went down the wrong hole." I rasped, wiping my fingers beneath my eyes.

"I hate it when that happens." Ashley sympathized, then turned her attention to where Ben was sitting. "There's a strange energy here." She was looking right at him, and I blinked in shock. *Could she see him?*

"Can she see me?" Ben clearly had the same thought.

"Like an astral glow." She continued, then ran a palm along her arm. "I have goosebumps." She did in fact have goosebumps along her arms, and the fine hairs were standing on end. Seems she couldn't see Ben, but she could certainly sense him.

"Ummm." I didn't know what to say.

"This energy is really attached to you, Audrey." Ashley's blue eyes were deadly serious. "There's a definite connection. Audrey? Are you being haunted?"

I coughed in surprise. "What?" Clearing my throat, I took another sip of coke, buying time to gather my scattered thoughts. "What makes you ask that?"

Ashley sat back in her chair, relaxing her shoulders, and laughed. "Sorry! That came across as totally crazy. It's just... I can see auras and there's an aura there." She pointed directly at Ben. "When there shouldn't be."

"Soooooo?"

"So that tells me there is a spirit present." Her smile widened. "I think it's Myra." Then she cocked her head. "I wonder if Myra has attached herself to you to help you solve her murder?" Before I could gather my wits to answer, she answered herself, clapping her hands in glee. "That must be it! How exciting."

I risked a glance at Ben, who was looking at Ashley with his mouth hanging open. Sensing my stare, he finally dragged his gaze away from the pretty young woman with the long, blonde dreadlocks by my side who could apparently see his aura and said. "Right. Weird. Anyway, as I was saying, bad news." I jerked my head a fraction to indicate he should continue. "Myra's gone."

"What?" I burst out, then quickly picked up my burger again and took another bite, trying to cover my sudden outburst.

"Yep. I don't know if she worked out how to leave her shop, or if she's gone into the light or whatever it is we're meant to do when we die." Ben continued. "But she's not there."

Ashley, thinking my blurted 'what' was directed at her, answered. "I'm sorry, that must have freaked you out, talking about spirits and ghosts and stuff."

"You believe in ghosts?" I asked, mouth full.

"Of course. And I think whatever presence is with us now is attached to you—your aura and theirs, they kinda blend in the middle." She was pointing from Ben to me, her finger doing a swirly motion between us. "Imagine it like a giant rubber band, connecting the two of you, stretching and flexing but never breaking."

"And you think this presence is Myra?"

"Who else could it be?"

Just as I shoved the last bit of burger into my mouth, a great big glob of ketchup splattered on my T-shirt. Brilliant. This day keeps getting better and better. Grumbling, I snatched up a napkin and began blotting, only all I achieved was to smear the stain further. I still had to ask mom about stain removal tips. Yet another mental note to add to my imaginary Rolodex.

I stood, tossing the napkin onto my plate. "Thanks for letting me gate crash your lunch," I said, pulling some bills from my wallet and placing them on the table. "That should cover it."

Ashley looked up at me, her smile angelic. She really was a sweet girl, I liked her. "It was good talking with you, Audrey. Come in soon for another massage."

"I will. That one you gave me worked wonders."

As I walked away Ben yapped in my ear. "Do you believe what she said? About the rubber band thing? That that's why I'm here, because I'm connected to you? That we're connected?"

Pulling out my phone, I pretended I had a call. "I don't know." I sighed. "It sounds plausible but I still don't get why or how."

"When this is over, you should tell her. Maybe she can help."

"Help?" I stumbled to a halt. "You don't want... this? To be here?" I'd never considered that, that Ben didn't want to linger on as a ghost, living on the fringes of existence. I blinked, the realization that I'd been undeniably selfish in wanting him to hang around suddenly dawning on me.

"What?" Ben darted in front of me to float along backwards when I began walking again. "Don't be crazy, Fitz. I'm not going anywhere. I'm not dissatisfied with my new life. It's just different is all."

"What did you mean by help then?"

"Well." He cleared his throat. "It would be neat if I could communicate with other people. Don't get me wrong, you're great! But when you're busy. Or sleeping. Or otherwise indisposed, it'd be nice to have someone else."

"Is that why you were excited about Myra? Because she was another ghost?"

"Yeah. And I can't help but worry about her. I hung about in her shop for ages, calling her name, waiting for her to turn up, but she didn't."

I'd never wanted to hug my best friend so badly. Seems it showed on my face because he frowned. "Shit. Fitz, I'm sorry, I didn't mean to bring you down."

"You didn't."

"I did. I'm an asshole."

"Well yeah, that's a given." I teased, lightening the mood. "I'm wondering if Myra has left the store and has attached herself to her boyfriend, Lee? I'm assuming this works because of the emotional bonds you and I share. So Myra and Lee must have powerful bonds too, and once she got over the shock of being dead, maybe it clicked into place?"

Ben was nodding. "Sounds like a plausible theory."

"One we'll check out later. Right now I'm going to swing by Jacob Henry's before heading home."

I'd reached my car when Ben growled. "You've got company." I turned to where he was looking to see a patrol car parked down the street.

Unlocking the door, I slid behind the wheel,

tossing my bag and phone onto the passenger seat, where Ben promptly appeared. I gave up chastising him for sitting his ghostly butt on my stuff.

"Relax. It's just a coincidence. That's not necessarily Mills' car and they could be here for official police business." I said. I didn't entirely believe it but was prepared to give the Firefly Bay PD the benefit of the doubt.

When I pulled out and the patrol car followed me I knew I was kidding myself. Hitting the indicator, I turned onto Kloeden Street, then made a right onto Pearl. Sure enough, the patrol car followed. I was one street away from Jacobs when the red and blue lights flashed.

"This is bullshit." Ben snapped.

"Couldn't agree more." I said, pulling over to the curb. Sure enough, it was Mills who swaggered up to my window. "Officer Mills. Twice in one day." My fake smile was getting a workout today.

"Tail light is out." He said.

"What? No, it isn't." Opening the door, I hurried to the rear of my car. Sure enough, the glass covering my right tail light was busted out. It hadn't been like that before I'd gone to lunch, which meant someone had broken it within the last hour. And I suspected that someone was standing right in front of me.

"Easy, Fitz." Ben warned, "he's baiting you. He wants this. He wants you to lose your shit, to incriminate yourself, to escalate the situation."

Ben was right. Whatever game Mills was playing, I was determined to stay out of it. Which meant I had to play my own game.

"Well, darn." I gasped, "it looks like you're right." I turned to Mills, batting my eyelashes. "I'm so sorry, I had no idea. I'll get that attended to right away."

He blinked, taken by surprise. "I'm going to have to write you up."

"Of course you are." I smiled through my teeth.

"Good, good," Ben said, hovering just behind Mills. "He's thrown. He was expecting a fiery reaction from you. Probably wanted an excuse to arrest you or something. Keep it cool. Take the fine, it's okay, we'll sort it."

"I'm so grateful you stopped me and pointed it out," I gushed. "The Firefly Bay Police Department doing their civic duty is something to be proud of."

"Jeez." Ben laughed. "Laying it on a bit thick aren't you, Fitz?"

Mills cleared his throat, tugging at the collar of his shirt. "Yes. Well. Make sure you get it repaired."

"I will. I promise." I took the fine and returned to the driver's seat, remaining stationary until the patrol car had pulled away. Once the taillights had disappeared, I gripped the wheel with clenched fists and yelled at the top of my lungs. "Son of a biscuit pea-brained stink shit!"

Ben laughed. "Feel better?"

"Much." Firing up the engine, I ran a soothing hand over the dash. "Do you think Mills broke my tail light?"

"Yup." Ben nodded.

"But why? Beside him being a turd that is."

"Have you riled him up lately? Got him off side?"

"No! That's just it. I avoid him as much as possible, I have done nothing to deserve this." Double checking that Mills hadn't driven around the block and was set to follow me again, I checked my mirrors, twice, before pulling out.

———

"Jacob Henry, you're a hard man to find." Resting one arm against his door jamb I studied the young banker who, despite being on a day off, was dressed in neatly pressed slacks and polo shirt, tucked in at the waist.

Jacob frowned, looked me up and down, then peered around me to see if I was alone. "Er, hi? You were at the bank when we were robbed, right? I saw your name on the telly later. Audrey something or other?"

I straightened up and smiled. "Audrey Fitzgerald." Holding out my hand I waited while he shook it, then held the door open wider, inviting me inside. You can tell a lot about a person by their handshake, and Jacob Henry's was like a wet fish. Limp and kinda gross. I wiped my palm on the back of my jeans.

"What can I do for you?" He asked.

His apartment was nice. A reasonable size, very neat. Emily Henry could have done much worse.

"I'm investigating the murder of Myra Hansen, the psychic down on the bay who owns Nether & Void."

Jacob's head dropped, and he ran a hand around the back of his neck. "Man, that was so awful what happened to her."

Ben walked through the wall and stood behind Jacob with his hands on his hips, head swiveling as he checked out the apartment. "Nice place." He nodded in apparent approval. I ignored him.

"So you were a regular of Myra's?" I prompted.

"Yeah." A flush of color swept up his neck and into his cheeks. Spinning on his heel, Jacob strode toward the kitchen, calling over his shoulder. "Coffee?"

"That would be great. Thanks!" While Jacob busied himself in the kitchen, I examined the living room. All in all it was very nice, if a little bland. Two matching bookcases stood either side of the big screen television and I wandered over to peruse the titles. It wasn't until I turned that something on the coffee table caught my eye. "Whoa." I said under my breath. Squatting, I peered closer at the cards spread haphazardly across the surface. Tarot cards. And I was pretty sure the design on the back matched the card I'd found under Myra's table.

"Oh."

I glanced up to see Jacob standing behind the sofa holding two cups of coffee, his face a picture of guilt.

"You take these from Myra's shop, Jacob?" I straightened. The flush of color in his cheeks darkened, and he nodded, reminding me of a puppy who'd been busted chewing his owner's slippers but it was impossible for you to be mad because of those eyes. "Did you kill her?"

He blanched. "What? No!" He hurried around the sofa to place the coffees on the table. I quickly backed away, putting an armchair between us. Just because he had puppy dog eyes did not mean he wasn't a murderer. Ben hovered close by, watching. I threw him a glance. A silent question. *Was I right to be cautious?*

"You know how Ashley can see auras?" Ben said. I nodded ever so slightly, keeping my attention on Jacob who had sunk onto the sofa and was now cradling his head in his hands. "Well, I can see... something. Something sticking to Jacob that has a stank to it."

"What?" I gave Ben my full attention. "A stank?"

Ben held his hands out, "I don't know how else to describe it. Like there's something dark sticking to him."

"Sticking? Like he's sat in something?"

"No." Ben threw his hands up in the air. "I don't know, it's like a soft-centered chocolate. From the outside it all looks normal, all nice, smooth chocolate, but on the inside you know there's something else. But you don't know what that something is until you bite into it."

"Unless you read the wrapper." I pointed out.

"There are no wrappers."

"Well, that's not hygienic. I wouldn't bite into a chocolate without a wrapper."

"Audrey, you're missing the point. On the inside —of Jacob—is a dark... blob. It's not big, it's not huge, but it's there."

"Kinda like when you step in dog poop?" I offered. "Because those little brown nuggets are small, but they pack a hell of a stink."

Ben grinned. "Yeah okay, kinda like stepping in dog poop. And that stank stays with ya all day."

"Gotcha." And then I realized I'd been conversing out loud with Ben and Jacob was watching me with round eyes, his hair standing on end where minutes ago his fingers had been pulling at the strands.

"You know," Ben continued, missing the fact that we had an audience, "now that I think about it, Regina Davis had her own stank going on. Not thick and dark like Jacob's, hers was more of a moldy orange type color, barely there. I didn't think much of it at the time."

Deciding the best way forward was to totally ignore the fact that from Jacob's viewpoint I was talking to thin air, I asked, "why do you have Myra's Tarot cards, Jacob?"

"I didn't kill her." Jacob repeated. I didn't believe him. The way his face kept changing color from mottled red to pasty white told me something was going on with him. Could be grief, I supposed, but was he really that attached to the psychic? He jumped to his feet, and I automatically took a step back. He froze. "Sorry. Sorry." He sank back onto the sofa. "I'm not going to hurt you."

"I don't think you need to worry." Ben said, hovering behind Jacob. "Remember when you took out Steven Armstrong? Jacob's smaller and lighter than him, you could take him no problem."

I remembered all right. Steven had thrown a punch, and I'd kneed him in the gonads in response.

He'd gone down like a sack of potatoes and had lay whimpering on the floor until Galloway turned up and arrested him. Ben was right. I could take Jacob if it came down to it. I rounded the armchair and sank down into it. "Tell me what happened."

Jacob was shaking his head, distress in his eyes. "I turned up for my appointment. The door was unlocked, like it always was." He sniffed, wiped his nose on the back of his hand. "I went in. The first thing I saw was the candle on the floor. Then Myra. Collapsed at the table. It wasn't until I got closer that I saw the knife sticking out of her back." He shuddered, sniffed, and looked at me with glassy, bloodshot eyes. Okay, so he didn't look like a killer, but you never know, he could be an exceptional actor. Leaning forward, I snagged one of the coffees.

"There's no sugar in that." Jacob warned me.

"That's okay. I'm sweet enough." I took a sip. I'd had worse. "What happened next?"

"I called the police. And then I saw the cards. They were scattered across the table in front of her. She must have been shuffling them when—" he choked, reached for his own coffee and took a gulp. "Before I even knew what I was doing, I scooped them up and shoved them in my pocket. Then the police arrived." There was an underlying edge of panic in Jacob's voice. I got it. He'd snagged the cards and then the police had arrived and it was too late to change his mind, too late to put them back because then he'd look as guilty as sin. So he took them with him.

"What I'm not understanding, Jacob, is why. Why take the cards?"

He looked up to the ceiling before bestowing those puppy dog eyes on me. "So I could use them myself. Myra had been reading the cards for me for so long that I figured I had a pretty good handle on how it all works. I thought—God, this is awful when I say it out loud—I thought, well, since she's dead she isn't going to need them and I could just... do it myself."

"Read the cards?"

"Yes." He sniffed, took another gulp of coffee.

"And why is that so important? That you have your cards read daily?" I remembered what his co-worker and Ashley had told me about his wife leaving him. Jacob confirmed it.

"To get Emily back. My wife."

"And how does having a card reading help with that?" I was truly curious because I wasn't seeing the connection.

Jacob opened his mouth to answer, then closed it

with a snap. "What?" I asked, watching a dazed expression cross his face. "What is it?"

"All this time... I thought... I thought the cards were helping me get my wife back..."

"Yeah? That's what you wanted, right?"

"Oh definitely. Emily is the most important person in my life, I love her so much it hurts. I don't understand why she stopped loving me." The puppy dog eyes were back tenfold. "But I think I just had an epiphany."

"Oh?"

"Having my regular readings with Myra were helping." He stated. "They were helping me. My self esteem. Myra had a way of making me feel good. She'd ask lots of questions about my life, she'd affirm I was doing the right thing, that I was strong, I was loyal."

"You're saying that the readings weren't about Emily at all? They were about you?"

He was nodding, his head bobbing up and down like a rowboat in rough seas. "She was teaching me to be a better man—" he snapped his fingers. "I see it now. She was making me a better man for Emily. So Emily would come back." With a grin, he flopped back, seemingly satisfied. It was my turn to frown. I wasn't sure that had been Myra's angle at all and that maybe Jacob was missing the point entirely.

"He's such a naïve little Muppet, isn't he?" Ben said, sitting on the arm of my chair. "I'd say our young Jacob Henry here as some sort of obsessive disorder. He's certainly obsessed with Emily. And if I were Emily, that level of utter devotion would get smothering pretty fast."

Excellent point. Another entry to my mental Rolodex. Speak with Emily Henry and find out the real reason she left her husband. I'd had her pegged as a shallow so-and-so, leaving her husband because he couldn't provide for her materially. Well, not at the level she wanted. Because this apartment? It was really nice. I'd find it odd that a woman left her husband because of an apartment like this.

I nodded at the cards. "I'm going to have to take those." I told Jacob. "And hand them over to the police."

"Yeah, I figured that." He rose, moving slowly so as not to startle me. "I'll get a bag to put them in."

As soon as he was out of earshot I whispered to Ben, "that stank that's stuck to him, do you think that could be an illness? Like he has some obsessive-compulsive type thing, and that's what you see?"

"I wouldn't say he has a compulsive order, not in

the OCD range, that's not reflected in his apartment at all. If he had OCD, the cards wouldn't be left in a mess like they are. And I've checked out the rest of his apartment. He's neat and tidy for sure, but I wouldn't say OCD."

"So his obsession is just with Emily? I wonder if there's a name for that."

"Psycho fits the bill." Ben muttered. "I'm going to check that he's not coming back with a knife."

I'd been fine until he's said that. Now I was worried Jacob had me fooled. I stood, moving behind the armchair once more while I waited for Jacob to return, sagging in relief when Ben called out, "It's okay, he's unarmed."

Jacob returned, and I watched while he gathered up the cards and shoved them into a zip-lock bag.

"How often did you see Myra?" I asked conversationally.

"Every few days." Jacob replied without looking up.

My eyebrows shot up. "I thought you saw her daily?"

"Nah. I saw her in person every few days and in between I'd get readings via her website."

"She has a website?" Rookie error, that should have been one of the first things I did when I took this case, research Myra Hansen. I'd remedy that as soon as I got home.

"Yeah, she gets a lot of business via her online portal."

With my mental Rolodex full to bursting, I thanked Jacob for his time and left, all without being murdered. Returning to my car, I put in a call to get the broken taillight repaired tomorrow morning, then headed home. A shower and change of clothes was long overdue. I hadn't missed the way Jacob kept eyeing the ketchup stain on my shirt, like he was itching to soak it in Vanish.

"*H*oly Hell." Ben whistled in my ear. We stood in the open doorway of my apartment, surveying the carnage inside. Someone had trashed my apartment. And I mean trashed. From my vantage point I could see the sofa had been torn to shreds, stuffing scattered around the room. It looked like every drawer and cupboard in the entire apartment had been pulled open and the contents dumped on the floor.

"No wait! Fitz, he's still in there!" Ben's warning shout came a second too late. I'd taken a step inside when a dark figure came barreling at me, charging past as he fled. I staggered back, my foot snagging on the lip of the doorframe. I couldn't stop my backward momentum, arms flailing as I tried to regain my balance and not end up on my backside. What I hadn't counted on was ricocheting into the railing running the length of the walkway outside and toppling over. The world spun crazily as I flipped through the air and over the side.

"Audrey!" Ben made a grab for my wrist, but passed right through me. I grabbed hold of the second railing, my body slamming into the side of the building with an oof. Dangling by one hand, I caught sight of the intruder pounding toward the staircase at the end of the building. Big man. Not fit, judging by his gate and the glimpse of a beer belly. Dressed in black sweats and a black hoodie that looked oddly bulky.

"Swing your other arm up." Ben commanded, crouched by the railing and leaning over to me. I did, managing to grab hold with both hands. Okay. Not going to die after all, but my shoulder was not thanking me for this extra beating it was taking. I managed to heave one leg up over the edge and pull myself up, rolling onto the walkway to lay on my back and stare up at the sky. "Are you okay?" Ben asked, sitting by my side, resting his hand on my arm.

"That was unexpected." I grinned, ignoring the icy chill of Ben's touch, needing the comfort it brought. That had been too close for comfort. Sitting up, I rolled my shoulders, wincing at the twinge. "I think I'm going to need another Ashley massage." I said. The oils she'd used, and her magic touch, had done wonders for my sore and bruised muscles after the car accident.

"I think you're going to need to call the cops." Ben said. He stood and disappeared inside to survey the damage. Using the railing, I pulled myself to my feet and joined him. Seeing my bag just inside the doorway where I'd dropped it, I rummaged inside for my phone.

"You know," Ben said, hands on hips, standing in the center of the room. "Whoever that was? They weren't here to steal anything."

"What makes you say that?" I was a little bit amazed at how calm I was, considering. I'd arrived home to find a thug destroying my home, then had accidentally thrown myself over the first-floor railing of my apartment building. I don't believe it had been the thugs intent to push me over the railing, he couldn't have known my sense of balance left something to be desired—or that I was the clumsy type who could trip over thin air—I was probably giving credit where it wasn't due, but anyway, I didn't think whoever had trashed my apartment had meant to harm me. Not physically. Otherwise, why break in while I'm not home? Why not wait until I am and then—what? Stick a knife in me? I shuddered, freaking myself out.

"It looks to me like he wanted to damage or destroy pretty much everything. It's like he was filled with rage. Even your mattress has been slashed. But your TV is still here, which let's face it, is pretty much the only thing worth stealing."

Ben was right. My belongings had been torn apart, quite literally. "You don't think they were searching for something?"

"Could be. But would you really go to the trouble and effort of tearing open a mattress? Like, what are you going to keep in there? All you need to do is look to see there's no stitch line where you'd sewn it back up. My take is that this is vandalism, pure and simple."

Phone in hand, I dialed the police and reported the break-in, then sat on the kitchen counter, Ben by my side, while I waited for them to arrive.

"You should call Kade." Ben said.

"Yeah." I should. I had his number on the screen when I heard booted feet outside.

"Police! Anyone here?"

Ben and I looked at each other. Of all the cops, it had to be Mills. What? He happened to be in the area? And this had to be the fastest response time from FBPD in history. He was obviously still following me. The big question was why? What had I done to deserve this vendetta?

"Yeah, inside." I called out, remaining seated on the countertop, watching warily when Mills appeared in my line of sight. His hand was resting on his gun as his eyes swept the room.

"Call Kade." Ben urged, nudging me in the ribs. I did, my finger hitting the call button.

Mills caught my movement the minute I put the phone up to my ear. "Put the phone down." He ordered. I ignored him. As far as I knew it wasn't illegal to make a call after you'd been burgled. Technically, I don't think I'd been burgled, just vandalized, but whatever, I'd call whoever I damn well wanted.

"Audrey, hi." Galloway answered just as Mills took a threatening step in my direction. It wouldn't have surprised me if he snatched the phone from my hand and ground it under his boot.

"Detective Galloway," I said, overly loud. Mills froze. Yeah buddy, I'm not the stupid dame you have me pegged for.

"What's happened?" Jeez, he was good. He knew, from the way I said his name, that things were far from okay. "Audrey, are you okay?"

"I'm fine." I assured him. "But there's been a break in at my apartment."

"Your apartment?" I could hear the puzzled tone in his voice. "Don't you live at Ben's house?"

"Yeah, no." I'd been meaning to tell him for quite some time that I wasn't actually living at Ben's, that I hadn't moved in yet, but the timing had never been right. And in the whole scheme of things, what did it matter anyway? "I haven't officially moved in yet."

There was a pause while he digested that. "Right. Okay. I'll be right there."

"Officer Mills is already here." I said.

"Hold tight. I'm on my way. Try not to knee him in the nuts."

"No promises."

15

*G*alloway arrived with reinforcements. Sergeant Addison Young stepped in behind him. "Holy heck, this place has been done over." She said. She crossed to Mills who was poking around over near my bed. "Find anything?" She asked him. He stiffened at her approach and a ruddy hue crept into his cheeks. "Negative."

Galloway crossed to my side. "How are you holding up?"

I gave him my most reassuring smile. I'm not sure if I pulled it off or if I was merely baring my teeth. "I'm fine."

"Tell me what happened."

I did. I noticed Sergeant Young stopped to listen,

but Mills got on rummaging around in my belongings. He wasn't even wearing gloves. Idiot.

"He was inside when you returned?" Galloway asked.

"Yes. I didn't realize that, of course. The door was open, I stepped inside and he came rushing out, knocking me out of the way. He ran off before I could stop him." Ben snorted at my omission of falling over the railing.

"And you're not hurt?" He pressed. I reflexively rolled my sore shoulder, wincing as the muscles protested. "I'm fine."

His eyes narrowed in on the movement. "You're not. You're in pain but too stubborn to admit it."

"True. Can we move on now, please?" I grinned. He sighed and shook his head. "What am I going to do with you, Fitz?"

"Well, you could help me gather up a few clothes to take to Ben's. Guess I'm going to be officially moving in."

"About damn time." Ben grinned.

"Sure." He held out a hand, and I placed mine in it, allowing him to help me down from the counter. I landed and stumbled into him, his hard chest halting my momentum, his grip on my hand firm. I allowed myself the small luxury of remaining leaning against him for a solid three seconds too long, but it was nice, leaning against him like this. He lowered his head so his mouth was next to my ear and whispered, "how long has Mills been here?"

"A while." I whispered back. "He got here really fast. Must've been in the neighborhood." I eased back, putting some space between us. "Some stuff happened today—I'll tell you about it later." My eyes shot to Mills, who was watching us. Galloway nodded, then turned. "What did you want to take?"

I surveyed my poor apartment. There wasn't much that hadn't been damaged, and since Ben's house came fully furnished, I didn't necessarily need to take anything other than my personal belongings. But I couldn't leave my apartment like this, my landlord would have a fit.

"I'll just take my clothes and toiletries for now and come back later to clear this lot out." It wasn't how I wanted this chapter of my life to end. A wave of nostalgia washed over me. I remembered picking up the old, battered dresser from a Trash 'n Treasure one windy Sunday afternoon. Ben and I had borrowed his dad's truck, heaved the dresser into the back of it and then lugged the darn thing upstairs to my apartment. Now its doors hung off and deep gouges scarred the wooden top. If I wanted too, I could probably have it repaired, find new doors for it, but the truth was, I didn't need it anymore. And that kinda made me sad.

"Lots of memories here, huh?" Galloway said.

"Yeah." Strengthening my resolve, I squared my shoulders and tipped my chin in the air. I'd known this day was coming. No use moping about it. Plus, it would be better for Thor if I was living in Ben's house permanently. I just hated that it had come about in such an awful way.

"Can I touch stuff?" I asked, my eyes scanning, searching for the one suitcase I owned. I couldn't see it, so I hoped it had survived in its hiding spot under my bed.

"Your prints will be on everything, anyway." Galloway nodded. "Sergeant, have the place dusted. I'll get Audrey to provide a list of any missing items."

"On it, Detective." Sergeant Young replied. She'd been busy snapping photos of the scene, something Mills had neglected to do. In fact, all Mills appeared to be doing was rummaging through my stuff. Ewwww.

"You own a hammer, Audrey?" Sergeant Young then asked. I snorted. "No." *Can you imagine? Me? With tools?* No, that was what Ben was for. If ever I

needed anything repaired, it was Ben to the rescue—
he came complete with his own toolbox.

Sergeant Young picked up something from the
floor between her finger and thumb and held it aloft.
A hammer. That's how the intruder had done so
much damage. He'd gone after my hard furnishings
with a darn hammer!

"Bag it." Galloway ordered, then rested a hand on
my shoulder. "Let's get you out of here."

You didn't have to tell me twice, because seeing
that hammer drove it home that whoever did this
was really, *really* angry with me and they wanted me
to know it. Message received. Only one tiny detail
was missing. Who, exactly, was angry at me? I had
no clue. It could be one of several people.

Given how small my apartment was, the unholy
mess, and four living adults, one ghost, it was
crowded to say the least. I elbowed past Mills to
retrieve my suitcase, heaving it onto the bed and
flipped it open. Packing was a matter of scooping up
armfuls of clothes and shoving them into said
suitcase.

I was in the bathroom, throwing my toiletries
into a shopping bag, when I heard Galloway berating
Mills. I stood and unashamedly eavesdropped.

"Mills!" Galloway barked. "Where are your

gloves? Jeez, man, how many years have you been a cop?"

"I'm out." Mills grumbled.

"Out? Of gloves? Why haven't you restocked your vehicle?"

"Haven't gotten to it yet. I'll do it when I get back to the station."

"Do it now. You can go. Young's got this, you can get back to traffic—after you've restocked." I didn't hear Mills' reply, but I felt the vibration of booted feet stomping across the floor, I cracked the bathroom door open and peeked outside. I could see Galloway and Young standing by the front door, examining where the intruder had busted it open. Mills was nowhere to be seen.

My phone buzzed, startling me, and I dropped the bag of toiletries. Fumbling for my phone I finally got it out of my pocket in time to see mom's name flash across the screen before it rang out. I hit re-dial.

"Oh, you are there." Mom answered. Then chuckled. "Drop your phone again? I was going to give you a couple of minutes and call back."

I laughed with her. It was a known fact in my family that I tended to drop my phone when it rings.

A lot. "Couldn't get it out of my back pocket." I explained.

"That's new." Mom chuckled.

"Not really. Anyway, glad you called… now I don't want you to worry—" I began, only to have her jump in, worrying. "What? What's happened? Are you alright?"

"Mom," I sighed, "what did I just say? Don't worry."

"I worry when you say stuff like that. Just tell me."

"There's been a break in at my apartment. It's okay, I wasn't home, but the place is a bit of a mess." Actually, the place was a lot of a mess, but I'd sugar coat it for my mom. "So I'm doing it. I'm finally moving into Ben's house."

My announcement was met with silence. Then she was off, a million words a minute. "That's wonderful! Not that you got broken into, no, that's not wonderful at all, that's awful. But you know your father and I worry about you living there, it's not the best neighborhood in the world." She sniffed. "But Ben's house is lovely. You'll be happy there. What do you need? Dad can bring the truck around. Brad and Dustin can help too." I'm sure my brother and brother-in-law appreciated being roped into helping me move. Not.

"Whoa, slow your roll." I protested. "I won't be taking any furniture—Ben's place comes fully equipped. But..." I chewed my lip. Mothers were worriers and mine was no different. "My apartment was kinda vandalized."

"Kinda?"

"Definitely. It was definitely vandalized."

"How vandalized are we talking? Smashed in walls?"

"No." Thank God. From what I could tell, no structural damage to the apartment itself. Just the contents. "I'm pretty sure every piece of crockery is broken." I eyeballed the kitchen where the cupboard doors stood open. Shards of broken cups, plates, and bowls littered the floor. "Someone had a hammer and went to town on my furniture. Ripped up the sofa and my mattress."

Mom sucked in a horrified breath. "That's awful!"

"Right?" I ran a hand around the back of my neck. I needed coffee. And that's when it hit me. "Oh my God!" I squeaked, rushing to the kitchen alcove, eyes searching frantically. But there it was, shoved to the back of the counter, untouched, unharmed. My Keurig.

"What? Audrey! What's happened now?" Mom's voice was frantic.

"It's okay," I soothed. "My Keurig is unharmed."

"You and that darn machine."

"It's my lifeline." I agreed. "But anyway, I thought maybe another family working bee? On the weekend, to clean this place up. Most of the stuff will need to go straight to the dump. I should hire a skip." My family had helped me clean Ben's house after the police had left it in a shambles after his murder, fingerprint dust everywhere. I hoped they wouldn't mind being used for manual labor again so soon.

"Of course, darling. Whatever you need."

"Thanks, mom." Then I remembered it was she who'd called me. "How are things with you? Everything okay?"

"Oh yes, all good. I was ringing to remind you we'd promised to go to Amanda's Yoga class tonight." Crap. We had. And by we, I mean my mom, myself, and my sister Laura. Amanda, my sister-in-law, had given us all yoga vouchers for Christmas and they were about to expire. As a paralegal at Beasley, Tate & Associates, Amanda kept immaculate records, and she knew we hadn't used the vouchers. A rather pointed conversation at last week's family dinner had reminded us of the fact.

"I hadn't forgotten." I protested. I had. I'd totally forgotten.

"Laura has offered to give us a lift. I'll tell her to pick you up from Ben's house."

"Yep. Fine. No worries." I eyeballed my overflowing suitcase. Did I have anything remotely suitable for yoga in there?

"The class starts at six. We'll swing by about quarter to. Be ready."

"I will, don't worry. I'll see you tonight then." I disconnected the call and looked at Ben, who was watching me with one of those constipated expressions again. Which usually meant he was trying not to laugh. "What?" I grumbled, shoving my phone back into my pocket. The following thunk behind me told me I'd missed, and it had slid down my leg to land on the carpet.

"You're going to… yoga?"

"So what?"

"You? The most uncoordinated person I know… yoga? Oh man, this I gotta see!"

I bent to pick up my phone. "You're not invited. Absolutely not."

"Uh, Fitz?" Ben jerked his head toward Galloway

and Young who were watching me from across the room, eyebrows practically in their hairlines, watching me talking to thin air. Friggin' perfect.

"What?" I sniffed defensively. "Is it a crime for a girl to talk to herself?"

"Smooth, Fitz. Smooth." Ben laughed. I shot him a look that told him if he were alive right now, I'd kill him.

"Everything okay?" Galloway asked, eyebrows settling into their rightful place.

"That was my mom." I explained. "Reminding me of yoga class tonight." Not that I needed to explain anything to him. Just that I was super aware of how absolutely friggin' insane I must look.

"Yoga?" The way he said it, as if I was nuts to even consider such a thing, had my hackles rising. What is it with the males in my life thinking it hilarious that I should take a yoga class?

"Just because I'm clumsy and uncoordinated doesn't mean I can't do yoga." I huffed, crossing my arms.

Galloway shook his head. "That's not what I'm getting at."

"No?"

"No. My concern is that you were in a vehicle roll over last night. And the way you're holding yourself

right now tells me you're in pain. Are you sure yoga
is such a good idea?"

"The doctor said gentle exercise was fine." Okay,
so he hadn't mentioned yoga specifically, but it
couldn't be that hard, could it?

16

"*O*kay ladies, let's walk the dog."

With my palms and feet flat on the yoga mat, and my butt in the air, I glanced up at the yoga instructor. What did walk the dog mean? I'd only just mastered downward dog.

"Now walk your feet in towards your hands and roll up through the body."

What? I'd missed walking the dog. Rather than roll up through the body, I shot upright, standing to attention, when I belatedly realized we weren't done yet. Oh no. Everyone else was standing with their hands together like they were praying. I quickly followed suit.

The instructor, Fliss was her name, continued. "Raise your hands and your face to the sun."

Whaaaat? We were inside. There was no sun.

"And fold down the body into a plank. Inhale and exhale, heart over the hands, into chaturanga, breathing into upward dog, and exhale into downward dog. Center yourself. Tell yourself *I am enough.*"

"I've had enough." I said under my breath. Laura, dangling upside down next to me, overheard and started to giggle, which made me giggle, and pretty soon the two of us had collapsed on the floor in a fit of laughter. Mom had lowered herself to her knees and was looking at us, her lips twitching, then she was in peals of laughter too.

"It's okay," Fliss said, "you're releasing emotion." At least she was smiling, not annoyed at us. Unlike Amanda, who was moving from pose to pose with practiced ease, all lithe and toned in her Lululemon yoga pants, her face a perfect mask of disapproval.

"Yoga is about releasing, letting go." Fliss continued, moving from pose to pose fluidly. "While building strength, flexibility, ease."

Laura, mom, and I got ourselves under control and attempted to resume the class, but what happened next slayed me. We were back in a downward dog, clearly Fliss' favorite pose, when Amanda farted. It wasn't a soft little toot either. It was a loud foghorn of a fart. I looked at Laura who was doubled over, clutching her stomach, body wracked with silent laughter. She turned her face toward me, and I could see tears streaming down her red face.

"We're releasing emotion," Laura struggled to get the words out, "and Amanda's releasing gas."

That was it. I was done. A wave of laughter engulfed me, I couldn't contain it, I laughed and laughed, laughed so hard I cried. The three of us, mom included, were a mess of hysteria. I vaguely heard Fliss saying, "Passing gas while practicing yoga is not unusual. You're moving your body in ways that will stir up your guts, which is a good thing."

I tried to get my mirth under control, I really did. Amanda was going to be so mad at us, but then I caught sight of her and she was laughing too and pretty soon the entire class joined in.

"Okay, ladies, let's wrap it up on such a happy note. Namaste." Fliss bowed.

"Namaste." We choked in reply.

I straightened and wiped my fingers over my wet cheeks, still chuckling. We returned our mats to the storage room, while Amanda rolled the one she'd brought with her and tucked it under her arm.

"You were pretty good for your first try." She said

to me. "With practice you'll find yoga will really help with your clumsiness."

I sucked in my lips, releasing them with a popping noise. I wasn't convinced yoga was for me. I hadn't found it particularly relaxing, or centering, or whatever else it was that I was supposed to get out of it. I hadn't even farted. Plus there was Amanda, trying to fix me. Again.

"But there was something I noticed, Audrey." Amanda reached out and tugged the hem of my T-shirt up. "What's this?"

"Hey!" I tried to slap her hand away, but she held firm, lifting the shirt high enough to reveal the bruise across my hips. "Quit it."

Laura and mom sucked in a shocked breath. "Audrey, what happened?" Mom touched my hip in concern.

"It's okay, I'm fine, it's just a bruise." Annoyed, I snatched the fabric from Amanda's fingers. She narrowed her eyes. "Correct me if I'm wrong, but that looks like a seatbelt bruise to me." She said.

"How would you know?" I snapped. Trust Amanda to ruin a perfectly good evening.

"Because I've seen plenty of photos from the motor vehicle accident cases my firm handles."

Oh. She was right, she probably saw plenty of photos with very similar bruises to mine. Darn it.

"Okay fine. I had a car accident. Happy now?"

She took a step back, hand to her chest, eyes wide, expression hurt. "Audrey! I'm only concerned that you're hurt, and that you didn't feel you could tell us."

"I didn't want to tell you because you'll all make a big fuss. Kinda like you're doing now." I'd known my family would find out eventually that I'd rolled Ben's car, but I'd hoped to delay the inevitable long enough for my bruises to fade.

"Have you been to a doctor?" Laura asked, rubbing a soothing hand up and down my back. She knew how I felt about Amanda. I loved my sister-in-law, I did, but Amanda was always trying to *fix* my clumsiness, resulting in me feeling like I was always less of a person around her. Damaged. It often put me on the defensive, and tonight was no exception.

I nodded. "Yes, I've been checked out and I'm fine. It's just bruising from the seat belt as Amanda pointed out."

"What happened?" Mom asked, glassy eyed.

"Oh, mom." I hugged her. "I'm fine, I promise. If I was really hurt I'd tell you. But I'm not, and you know how I bruise. There isn't a day gone by when I don't add another to the collection."

Like today, for example, when I'd fallen over the railing and slammed into the wall. Both knees now sported fresh bruises. But again, that wasn't something I'd choose to share with my family, especially with Amanda here, for she'd double down her efforts on trying to fix me. That was what this yoga class had been about after all, no matter that she'd disguised it as a gift for all of us.

"It was my own fault. I was driving Ben's Nissan, took a corner too fast, and it rolled." All three women sucked in their breath.

"You rolled it?" Laura asked, eyes huge as saucers. I nodded. "I'm devastated about it. I loved that car. But I guess I wasn't used to driving it, what with a higher center of gravity and all." Part truth, part lie. I figured it best to leave out the fact that the reason I was driving so fast in the first place was because I was being chased by bad guys who were shooting at me.

Mom slung an arm around my shoulders and squeezed. I hid my flinch. If they thought the bruises across my hips were bad, they should see my shoulder. But that's why I'd worn a T-shirt to yoga, rather than a tank top. To hide the mottled purple and black marring my skin.

"You've had an awful couple of days, love."

I sighed. Truer words had never been spoken. They didn't know about the harassment from Officer Mills, the trumped-up charges. And I was pretty sure he'd broken my taillight just so he could book me for it. I was also convinced he'd responded to my break in call so fast because he'd been stalking me, probably patrolling around and around my block waiting to flag me down for some other made up transgression. But all of that, I kept to myself.

"Not that this hasn't been fun, but we should get going, we're the only ones left." I pointed out. The surrounding room had emptied while I'd faced the Fitzgerald family's version of the Spanish inquisition.

"Actually, I found it quite cathartic." Laura looped her arm with mine and together we headed toward the door. "The laughter that is." She added. "I haven't had a good laugh like that in ages... I feel better for it."

"Same." I smiled. She was right. It had been cathartic and like Laura, I too felt better than when I had before class, only it had been because of letting loose in uncontrollable laughter, not the yoga itself.

"So glad you enjoyed it." Amanda beamed, turning to flash her pearly whites at us while she walked ahead. "Does this mean you'll be joining me for regular classes?"

"Doubtful." Laura said under her breath, nudging me in the ribs.

"I'll think about it." I said, loud enough for Amanda to hear. Laura swung her head. "Really?" She whispered. I shook my head. Nope. I wasn't a massive fan of exercise in any form and trying to follow tonight's class had been stressful. By the time I got myself into the right pose, Fliss had moved on to the next. I felt like I'd been constantly two poses behind the entire class. Let's not talk about balancing. Anything on one foot was my downfall. Literally.

We were out in the carpark, heading toward Laura's people mover when I glimpsed movement out the corner of my eye. In the far corner of the lot were a man and woman, kissing passionately, pressed up against a red sports car. I paused. The woman looked familiar.

"Tsk." Amanda said, stopping by my side and watching the couple. "Those two are at it again."

I peered closer. "Is that? Is that Regina Davis?" I couldn't believe my eyes. Regina Davis was pashing someone who I was pretty sure wasn't her husband, not by the way her hands were clenching his ass and pulling him close. This guy didn't kiss like a gay man kissing a woman. Not that I'd know, but I assumed a gay man would not be all over a woman like this guy was all over Regina.

"You know her?" Amanda asked, then continued without waiting for an answer. "She's been hooking up with her gardener for a while now. Tells her husband she's coming to yoga and instead meets Juan in the parking lot and they head off in his truck. Probably to some seedy hotel that charges by the hour."

"Is this common knowledge? Like... an open secret?" I was thinking how everyone seemed to know that Regina's husband was having a long-term relationship with his male secretary so wouldn't bat an eye at Regina having a little fun of her own.

Amanda shrugged. "I don't know. I've seen them a few times. Other people may have as well, but I haven't heard anyone gossiping about them if that's what you mean."

Laura tooted the horn of her people mover. "You coming? Or catching a lift with Amanda?"

"I'm coming!" I hurried to jump in the back seat, squeezing in between baby seats, all the while thinking about Regina Davis and her secret affair. It wasn't exactly a motive for murder. Not unless Myra knew about the affair and was threatening to blab. Or maybe blackmail her. I really needed to have another chat with Myra.

Mom and Laura dropped me home, my new home, previously known as Ben's house.

"Amanda meant well." Mom said, kissing my cheek.

"I know mom. She always does."

"I'll round up the troops and we'll sort out your apartment on Saturday."

"Thanks mom. You're the best."

Laura tooted the horn, and drove off while I unlocked the door and let myself in.

"About time!" Thor greeted me. "I'm starving."

I'd come to learn that his complaints that imminent death from starvation was actually Thor showing his relief that I'd turned up at all, that he'd missed me. I ruffled the fur on top of his head. "Hey, buddy. Miss me?"

He trotted ahead of me, tail straight up in the air, much like a one finger salute. I chuckled. Yep, if Thor could flip me the bird, that would be it.

"How did yoga go?" Ben asked. I'd forbidden him

to come and after much arguing he'd finally agreed to stay put with Thor.

"It was as you'd expect. Laura, mom, and I got the giggles." I smiled at the memory. "Oh, and Amanda farted."

"Amanda?" Ben snort laughed. "She wouldn't have liked that!"

"Actually, she wasn't fazed at all. But then she's been doing yoga for years, so it probably wasn't the first time she dropped one in class." I dropped my bag at the end of the sofa and headed into the open-plan kitchen, making a bee-line for the coffee machine. Correction. My Keurig, which now sat alongside Ben's fancy, complicated, machine.

"Oh, and get this. I caught sight of Regina Davis in a compromising position with her gardener."

"Compromising position? What, as in… yoga?"

"No silly. They were kissing in the parking lot. Amanda tells me she's seen them before, that Regina pretends to go to yoga, leaves her car in the lot and takes the gardener's truck to some hotel."

Ben opened his mouth to reply, but the doorbell ringing had him snapping it shut again. Before I could so much as blink he was off toward the front door, sticking his head through it to see who was on the doorstep.

"It's Galloway. You're going to like this." His grin was wide as he stepped back, allowing me to pass without coming into contact with his icy visage.

"Like what?" I asked, then opened the door to find Galloway standing there with a pizza box balanced on one hand, a six-pack in the other.

"I took a gamble you haven't eaten." He said by way of greeting. Ben was right. I liked this. A lot.

"You better come in, detective."

17

*Y*ou know what's better than beer and pizza? Having someone serve you beer and pizza. Galloway waved me to the sofa and told me to put my feet up while he served up the food. I could see Ben getting twitchy that we were eating on the sofa and not the dining table and I shot him a wink and a silent promise to try not to get pizza sauce on the cushions.

"How was yoga?" He asked around a mouthful of pizza.

"As expected," I replied, taking a swig of beer. "I wobbled all over the place like a newborn foal trying to find his legs for the first time."

Galloway smiled. "And the shoulder?"

"How do you even know my shoulder has been

bothering me?" I reflexively rolled the shoulder in question, wincing at the answering twinge. Yep. Still hurt.

"Because you pull that face whenever you move it." He said drolly. Standing up, he gathered our dirty plates and stacked them in the dishwasher, rummaged around in the freezer, then returned with a bag of frozen peas.

"Uh. No thanks."

He snorted. "It's for your shoulder. Next best thing to an ice pack." He pressed it against my shoulder and I automatically put my hand over his to hold it in place. That sizzle was back, the one wherever my skin came into contact with his, and a spark ignited. I'm surprised we didn't defrost the peas. Slowly he eased his hand out from beneath mine and resumed his seat. I tried not to let my disappointment show on my face.

Ben snorted and started making kissy faces behind Galloway. I ignored him.

"You said some stuff happened today?" Galloway said, reminding me of what I'd whispered to him in my apartment.

"Yes. It's Mills. I think he's following me. He pulled me over twice today and ticketed me both times. One for using my cell phone while driving.

FYI I wasn't! But it's effectively his word against mine." I shrugged, the peas crinkling in my ear. "Then when I came back to my car after lunch, my taillight was all busted out and he ticketed me for that."

"You think he broke it?" Galloway didn't even sound surprised.

I nodded. "There's no other damage, like if someone hit me, they'd have been scrape marks on the paintwork or something, surely. And then the break in? He was there really fast, like he was waiting right out front."

"I'll look into it." He glanced around. "This place has an alarm system, doesn't it?"

"Yeah. Why? You think I'm in danger?" I was shocked. Mills was being a dick, sure, but would he take it that far?

"I'm saying you need to watch your back. Yesterday someone was shooting at you. Today your apartment was broken into. And I'd sleep better knowing you were safe." My mind drifted to visions of Galloway sleeping, wondering if he slept nude, picturing him spread out across a bed, a sheet tucked tantalizing low on his hips.

"Awwwww." Ben drawled, "isn't that sweet."

"Do you think they're related? The shooting and

my apartment? Is this all tied back to the bank robbery?" I jerked my mind out of the bedroom and back to the topic at hand. Then I remembered something else. I'd been to visit Jacob and had the tarot cards in my bag. Jumping up from the sofa, I grabbed my bag and dug them out, holding them out to Galloway. "I almost forgot. Well, I did forget, but anyway, I've remembered now. I dropped by Jacob's place after lunch, and he was home. These were spread out over his coffee table."

Galloway accepted the zip-lock bag. "Myra's tarot cards?"

"Yep. He confessed to pocketing them. He figured he could continue the readings at home, himself. Oh, and get this, he wasn't seeing Myra every day. Apparently she had some sort of website where you could get readings online."

"Yeah, forensics cracked her laptop today. We know all about her website."

"What did you find?" The way he said it, like it was something ominous, had me sitting on the edge of the sofa in anticipation.

"It turns out Myra is a fraud. She's set up shell companies in Thailand, Switzerland and Monaco, leaving a complicated business web we're still unraveling. She has dossiers on all of her clients and a lot of other citizens that we assume she intended to target."

My eyes shot to Ben, who stiffened at Galloway's words. Now I really needed to speak with Myra and find out what the hell she was playing at. Seems Ben had the same idea for he started doing some sort of sign language, which was crazy because Galloway couldn't see or hear him. But I got the gist of it. He was ducking out to go find Myra. At least I assumed that was what all the finger twirling and pointing and two fingers walking was all about.

"Meaning if any of her clients found out, they could be the killer." I said.

"That's why I got called back to the station. The Chief wants this one closed as quickly as possible. Myra has left a trail across the country of duped clients. Only she hid her tracks very well." He lapsed into silence, watching me.

"What?" I squirmed, uncomfortable with his intense stare.

"Your turn. I've shared what I know, now it's your turn, because I know you found out something today, you're as twitchy as a squirrel on crack." Oh my God, he even used my own sayings. This guy was in my head and I wasn't sure I liked it. Or loved it.

I cleared my throat. He had a point, and after all,

he was my supervisor until I got my PI license. "A couple of things." I told him about Regina lip locking with her gardener in the yoga studio parking lot. And then my lunch with Ashley, and how Lee, Myra's boyfriend, had unexpectedly left as soon as I joined them.

"Regina alibied out." Galloway said. "She had an early morning PT session, confirmed with her trainer, Jayden Ellis, just like she told us. Then she met a friend, Klara Hill, for breakfast at the Seaview Café. CCTV footage puts her at the café from eight thirty until just after ten."

"Okay." I chewed my lip, thinking. "You know we can't rule out Ashley Baker. Just because she hired me to find Myra's killer doesn't mean she can't be the murderer. Her sister is doing time for drug smuggling."

"Yeah? What's her sister's name, I'll look into it."

"Skye. But she's claiming she was set up by her boyfriend, a guy called Rhys Parker. This was back in Portland. Actually no, Skye is in jail in Nassau. Oh, and get this!" I snapped my fingers, remembering what Ashley had told me. "This Rhys guy used to work with Lee, Myra's boyfriend!"

Galloway leaned forward, resting his elbows on

his knees, eyes intent. "I don't want you questioning Lee Noble."

"What! Why?" He was next on my list. If my place hadn't been trashed today, I would have sought him out this afternoon.

"He has a record."

My eyes rounded. "What did he do?" I breathed.

Galloway ticked off on his fingers. "Possession of a controlled substance. Possession of stolen property. Trespass." He paused for a moment, rubbing his chin. "I have an idea. Can I use your computer?"

Surprised, I nodded. "Yeah, sure." My laptop was still wrapped in a bundle of clothes and shoved in my suitcase, which was yet to be unpacked in the guest bedroom—I couldn't bring myself to use the master suite. That was Ben's room and while I'd finally moved into his house, I wasn't ready to take over his bedroom. I hadn't even packed up his clothes and belongings, despite mom offering to help me a dozen times now. "We'll have to use the one in the office, mine's still packed."

Galloway followed me into the office and stood watching while I booted up Ben's computer. I know I needed to stop thinking of everything in terms of Ben. Ben's house. Ben's computer. Ben's sofa. All of it was mine now, but I was still coming to terms with it. Baby steps, I told myself, baby steps.

Galloway took the chair, and I stood watching over his shoulder while he pulled up the internet browser, then logged in to the FBPD server.

"I didn't know you could do that." I said.

"You can't. Not usually. But I knew Ben's computer would have a token, allowing remote access. I had a hunch the FBPD IT guys never got around to revoking it." He began typing, fingers flying across the keyboard. I was impressed that he could touch type and wasn't finger pecking. Then a photo of Lee Noble popped up on the screen. A mug shot. He looked mean, his eyes scowling at the camera.

"What are you looking for?"

"Known associates."

"Why?"

"You said it yourself. Ashley Baker may have hired you to avoid suspicion. Her sister is in jail. You interrupted her having lunch with Lee, who left when you arrived. And it was Ashley who told you that her sister's boyfriend used to work with Lee."

"You think she's deflecting? Giving us false leads?"

"Maybe. Maybe not." He was scrolling through

Lee's rap sheet when he paused. "Here we go. Rhys Parker."

"Apparently Rhys told Skye that they'd won this radio competition, a vacation to the Bahamas. Skye was arrested when customs found drugs hidden in the lining of her suitcase. Ashley thinks Rhys framed her, that he was using her as a drug mule. When Rhys was released after questioning and flew home, it was Lee who picked him up from the airport. Although according to Ashley, Lee claims he only did it as a favor for a co-worker." I told him.

"Well, this says different. Rhys Parker and Lee Noble were both arrested for possession of a controlled substance. Cocaine. Both spent a year in jail eight years ago."

"So they knew each other. It wasn't just a work thing."

"Affirmative."

"Do you think Lee could have killed Myra? I don't get what motive he'd have. According to Ashley, he was all set to propose to her."

"Maybe he did, and she said no?"

"She wouldn't have said no. Ashley said it was Myra who was all excited that some big changes were coming, and she was just waiting on Lee."

Galloway was silent for a moment, drumming his

fingers on the desk. "What if the big changes weren't a marriage proposal? We know Myra was a fraud, a crook. And Lee has a criminal record."

I clapped a hand over my mouth, then slowly peeled away my fingers as realization dawned. "The bank robbery! What if they were behind the bank robbery?"

Galloway nodded. "It's a possibility. Lee works at the docks. The van disappeared at the docks. You were shot at, at the docks. Then today you're sniffing around and then your apartment is trashed."

"You think it was Lee?" But I frowned, recalling the intruder who'd pushed me out of the way. Lee had reeked of cigarette smoke. The intruder hadn't. Lee was a tall guy, the intruder, not so much. I told Galloway my observations.

"He could have sent someone else. There were two other men involved in the robbery. And the getaway driver." He reminded me.

A light bulb went on in my head, and I snapped my fingers. "What if Myra was the getaway driver? And, and," I rushed in excitement, "Jacob was the inside man. They had to have someone on the inside, otherwise how would they have known about that big delivery of cash was due!"

"We really do need to talk to Jacob Henry."

Galloway said, pushing back the chair and standing up.

"Now?" I was surprised, it was after seven, didn't he need to clock off or whatever.

"No time like the present." He was halfway out the door when he suddenly stopped and turned to me. I hadn't been expecting it, so I ran into him, bouncing off his chest. He caught me before I ended up on my ass on the floor. "Sorry." He said, making sure I was steady on my feet before releasing me. "I should have checked."

"Checked what?"

"That you're up to it. That you're not too tired?"

His thoughtfulness took me by surprise. Today had been a long day, and I was utterly wiped out. "I'm fine." I lied through a bright smile.

He nodded and swiveled on his heel, muttering under his breath, "as if you'd tell me if you weren't." I almost snorted. Galloway was getting to know me a little too well.

18

When Jacob opened the door and saw me standing there with Galloway, I thought he was going to faint. All the color drained from his face and he clutched the door frame, holding himself upright.

"May we come in?" Galloway asked, flashing his badge.

"Sure." Jacob croaked, releasing his death grip on the door frame and staggering to the sofa where he flopped as if his legs wouldn't hold up another second.

"Are you here to arrest me?" He asked, voice glum. Defeated.

"Do I need to?" Galloway asked, nodding that I should take a seat. I cautiously moved behind the sofa and perched on the same armchair I'd occupied earlier in the day. There was something about Jacob that made me uneasy.

"I took the Tarot cards. From Nether & Void." He swung his eyes towards me. "You told him, right?"

"I did." I nodded.

"We are going to need to talk about that, yes." Galloway told him. "But first I want to know about your relationship with Myra Hansen."

"Relationship?" He jerked in surprise. "I'm not having a *relationship* with her. She's my psychic."

"I didn't mean a romantic liaison." Galloway clarified. "I want to know what the two of you talked about."

A wave of red washed over Jacob's cheeks. "I already told her." He nodded in my direction. "Myra was helping me get my wife back."

"Outside of the readings." Galloway pressed. "You know, general chit chat. When you first arrive and sit down and she asks how are you, that type of thing. What did you talk about?"

Jacob looked confused. Then concerned. He made that face that Ben often gets, the one that looks like he's constipated and really, badly, needs to poop.

"Oh God." He whispered and buried his face in

his hands. I glanced at Galloway, thoroughly confused.

"Jacob? Were you feeding information to Myra about the bank?"

Seconds ticked by, the only sound was Jacob's harsh breathing, then he lifted his head from his hands, his eyes glassy with unshed tears. "I think I may have." He whispered.

"Tell me." Galloway ordered.

"It wasn't intentional." Jacob hurried to assure us. "She had a way of getting you to open up, to tell her things you wouldn't ordinarily tell people. And she'd ask how work was, what my career aspirations were, that type of thing."

Galloway and I shared a glance. He'd told me she was good, and this confirmed it. I could see how, over time, she'd get clients to reveal all their secrets.

"It wasn't until after the robbery, and the police were questioning everyone and asking us—the staff— if we'd told anyone about the scheduled delivery and I'd said no, because I didn't think I had, but then later I got to thinking about it and I realized that I may have mentioned it to Myra, but it was just in passing, an offhand comment about a busy day at work coming up due to the delivery. I was going to ask Myra about it at my next reading, because I wasn't one hundred percent sure I had." He held out both wrists to Galloway. "Go ahead. Arrest me. This is all my fault."

"I'm not going to arrest you." Galloway said. "But you are going to need to come down to the station for a formal interview. And we still need to chat about you swiping evidence from a crime scene."

Jacob dropped his arms. "Right. Yes. Okay." Then he looked down at his clothing, which was immaculately ironed. "Can I get changed first?"

"Go ahead."

Once he'd left the room I leaned toward Galloway and asked, "are you going to tell him she's a fraud? That everything she told him is a big bag of baloney?"

He inclined his head. "Yeah. I'll fill him in at the station. My gut instinct is he's not directly involved. Myra used him. She may have targeted him intentionally, as a source of information for the bank, or it could have been coincidence but once she learned of his connection to the bank, I'd say she quickly hatched a plan to use the connection."

"I guess we'll never know." I sighed.

"Oh, we'll find out. Now we know what we're looking for, I'll get Collier or Walsh, whoever's on duty tonight, to search her records for Jacob's file.

She'll have one on him, and it will all be spelled out in black and white. Lucky for us Myra kept detailed records on her victims, including her intentions and plans on how she'd either blackmail them or trick them into giving her money for fake investments. She'd have had a plan for Jacob."

"But she clearly wasn't working alone. Because the men who held up the bank were, well, they were men. Not one of them was a woman. Which brings us back to the getaway driver. Do you think it was Myra?"

"One thing about robberies. The more people involved, the smaller the cut of the spoils."

"So if Myra is the mastermind—and we're assuming she is—then the bounty would be split between her, the three men who held up the bank, and the driver. But if she was the driver, then it only needed to be split four ways, instead of five."

"Exactly."

"Then running with that..." I chewed my lip as I thought through the bank robbery scenario in my head. "What's to say it wasn't one of the robbers who killed Myra for her share? Maybe they were pissed that they hadn't got the big jackpot she'd promised? Rather than split the spoils between four, off the competition and then you only have to split it between three."

"Wouldn't be the first time it's happened."

"I'm ready." Jacob interrupted, having changed from his immaculate casual clothes to a suit. His earlier pallor was gone, and he held himself with confidence rather than the timid, scared young man he'd been mere minutes ago. Galloway's gut may have been telling him Jacob was an innocent in all this, but my gut wasn't convinced.

"Wow. A suit." Galloway eyed him up and down. "Okay, let's go."

Galloway had set me up in the observation room, where I could watch the interview with Jacob on a monitor. So far we hadn't learned anything new, merely confirmation of what Jacob had already told us. I'd gone in search of coffee and had been eyeballing the vending machine in the corridor when a commotion at the front desk drew my attention. Poking my head around the corner, I saw a young blonde woman at the counter demanding to see her husband.

"Emily?" Taking a guess, I approached. Her head

snapped around. "Yes? Do you have Jacob? This jackass won't let me see him. I demand to see him. Now." She stamped her foot to emphasize her point. Yeah, like that is going to work.

"Hi, Emily, I'm Audrey, why don't you come and have a seat." I placed a hand on her back and guided her to the chairs lining one wall. I shot the officer behind the counter a look, hoping he'd read it correctly. He nodded in return, which I hoped meant he'd get a message to Galloway that Jacobs' estranged wife had turned up.

"Where is he?" She demanded, her agitation obvious. I placed what I hoped was a soothing hand on her arm. "He's just answering some questions right now."

"About what? That stupid psychic he was seeing? All of this is her fault." She sniffed.

"Wait. Was he seeing Myra before you left?"

She nodded. "He started seeing her when I didn't get pregnant immediately."

I blinked in shock. "Okay, Emily, tell me everything. From the beginning."

She slumped back against the hard plastic chair. "Look, Jacob can be a difficult person to live with. I knew that going in. He's incredibly possessive and intense and likes everything to go according to plan.

When things go off course, it's like…" she paused and looked up at the ceiling. "It's like someone with OCD who has to check three times that the door is locked."

"Does he have OCD?" I remembered Ben saying he didn't think that was the case. Emily shook her head. "No. But we had an appointment to see someone about his mental health. And then Myra got involved."

She turned her head to look at me. "I love my husband. I do. Despite all the rumors and gossip that I only married him because I wanted a big fancy wedding."

"Why did you leave then?"

"Because of Myra. She tapped into something with Jacob. Swayed him to do things that I don't think he would have done if it weren't for her suggestions."

"Such as?"

"We had a plan, and I was totally okay with it. We were on track for buying our own place, had a nice deposit saved and we'd agreed we'd start trying for a baby, that there's enough room in the apartment to raise one child, but we'd be in a house before we tried for a second. And you and I both know you don't necessarily become pregnant the first time you try. So when my period arrived, Jacob… he needed answers, and I refused to go to the doctors and have needless fertility tests done because we'd only just started trying. But he couldn't let it go. Then he found her. A bloody psychic."

"And before you know it, he's chewing through our house deposit money to pay her! And she's telling him all of these conception secrets. Utter nonsense, and for an intelligent man it surprised me he couldn't see through her. Stuff like, I had to sleep on the left side of the bed. That I had to wear the color purple. That I had to hold my glass in my left hand when drinking. Then it all started to get a bit much. He's planning my meals, monitoring my diet, where I go, who I see. He's calling or messaging me constantly. I had to turn my phone off while I was at work because of the constant interruptions. He intruded into every waking moment of my life. So I left. I went home to stay with mom and dad for a while until he could get his head on straight."

"When was this? How long had he been seeing her before you left?"

"About a month, give or take."

I thought about what she'd told me. Jacob had started seeing Myra before his wife had left him.

Had she known then that she could use him? That he could be of use to her?

"Did you ever go see her with him? Like a couple's session?"

"Pft. No. Our last fight, before I left, I demanded he not see her anymore, that it was her or me and he said he wouldn't choose, that Myra gave him guidance and a path. A plan. And his personality dictates that he always has a plan. He needs structure. That's why I wanted him to see a psychiatrist. Because I know his brain isn't wired the same as most people's and we needed a way to make it work, for both of us. Myra convinced him he didn't need to keep that appointment."

"Is he violent? Has he ever hurt you?"

Emily's eyes rounded. "Never! Jacob couldn't hurt a fly. Like, seriously. He'll catch them and release them out the window. Jacob doesn't so much as get angry, he gets... intense. That's why his behavior reminds me of OCD in some ways. Instead of getting angry, he'll start obsessively cleaning or rearranging the pantry or the closet."

"Emily?" Jacob and Galloway appeared. Emily jumped to her feet and rushed into her husband's arms. "Baby! Are you okay?"

He wrapped his arms around her and buried his

face in her hair. "I've missed you so much." He whispered.

I crossed to Galloway. "Erm. How did she even know he was here?"

"I may have let him make a phone call. He was convinced he was under arrest."

"He's not, is he?"

Galloway shook his head. "Jacob is another of Myra's victims. While I was interviewing him, Walsh dug through the data forensics unearthed earlier and he found the file on Jacob. Under a code name, of course. But she had him pegged from the first visit, and her plan was nasty. Drive a wedge between Jacob and his wife, because she knew that as soon as Emily got pregnant, Jacob wouldn't have a reason to see her anymore. She needed to give him a reason. So get rid of the wife. Then Jacob's obsessive nature would demand that he see her to help him get his wife back, for there was one thing about him that she knew would keep him under her thrall. His love for his wife."

"That's so calculated. And mean." I shuddered. Then a thought popped into my head. "You don't think Emily…" I trailed off.

"While I couldn't blame her if she had killed

Myra, it wasn't Emily. She alibied out, she was in the city for a job interview."

"She was planning on leaving town?" I swiveled to look at the young couple currently entwined in each other's arms.

"Maybe it was too painful for her to stay?" Galloway suggested.

"Maybe." Watching them now I couldn't help but smile. Judging by all the touching and goofy expressions, Emily and Jacob were now reconciled. At least something good has come out of this whole sorry situation.

19

*O*fficer Walsh waylaid Galloway before we could leave. I waited for what felt like a hundred hours, sitting on the hard plastic chair in the foyer, the sorry excuse they called coffee in the vending machine doing nothing to keep me awake. I may have been dozing, my chin resting on my chest, a slow pool of drool growing on my T-shirt when two warm hands landed on my knees. I jerked awake, cracking my head against Galloway's as he crouched in front of me.

"Ow." I rubbed my forehead and squinted at him.

"This brings back memories." He too was sporting a red mark on his forehead. "Just don't move, okay? Last time we bumped heads you almost took me out completely."

"As if." It was true, I remembered our meeting, how he'd saved me when I'd stumbled off the curb and into the path of an oncoming bus. He'd pulled me out of harm's way, but I'd swung around and not only did our heads collide, I'd accidentally hit him in the nuts.

I yawned. "What time is it?"

"Just gone ten. Sorry to keep you waiting."

"S'kay." I yawned again. God, I was tired. "You ready now?" We'd taken Galloway's car, so I was stuck at the station until he was ready to leave. Which was hopefully now? Then I caught the remorseful expression on his face, and my heart sank.

"I'll get Officer Walsh to drop you home." He offered.

"Don't tell me something's come up?"

He hunched his shoulders. "Sorry."

"Don't be." I patted his knee. "Crime never sleeps, right?" That's what Ben used to say, and I figured it was a cop thing. Plus, it wasn't wrong. I glanced over Galloway's shoulder at Officer Noah Walsh approaching. "Ready, Audrey?" he asked. I consoled myself with the fact that Officer Walsh was an okay guy and I figured Galloway must've thought so too, otherwise he'd never have arranged for him to give me a lift.

"Yup." I tried to stifle another yawn, my eyes watering in protest.

Galloway stood and extended a hand, helping me to my feet. I could practically hear my bones cracking and creaking, protesting each movement. Then I remembered something important. I had now, officially, moved into Ben's house. And the master bathroom had a bath! With my enthusiasm on the rise, I pictured a hot steaming soak in my immediate future.

Galloway leaned down and planted a kiss on my cheek, taking me by surprise. His lips burned a hot trail from my cheek to my ear, where he whispered, "don't forget to set the alarm." Not the sexiest words ever whispered in my ear, but still, his hot breath dancing across my skin had me tingling from head to toe, my previously sluggish body now fully awake and alert.

"Right." I croaked, then cleared my throat. "Set the alarm."

I followed Officer Walsh out the door towards his squad car, casting a quick glance back over my shoulder. Galloway stood where I'd left him. Watching. He raised his hand in salute and I smiled, before Officer Walsh distracted me by stopping and I walked straight into him.

"Offf. Sorry." I staggered back, only just managing to keep my footing.

"You okay?" he asked, holding open the passenger door. God, I'd been so distracted ogling Galloway that I hadn't even realized we'd reached the patrol car.

"Yeah, sorry again. Occupational hazard with me, I'm afraid." I slid inside and pulled my seatbelt on.

"Heard you had a bit of trouble at your apartment." Walsh said as he gunned the engine and nosed the car out of the lot.

"You could say that." I'd successfully managed to push the whole sorry affair to the back of mind but now it was looming forefront once more and a shiver danced over my skin. At least I'd be safe at Ben's house, and I'd have him and Thor to watch out for me, not to mention the alarm.

"Detective Galloway asked me to take a look around when I drop you off, make sure everything is secure."

"Oh. Right. Thank you."

"All part of the service."

We spent the rest of the drive in silence, which was fine with me. Pulling up in the driveway, Walsh killed the engine, then preceded me up the path to the front door, helpfully shining his flashlight while I dug out my keys. Pushing open the door with Walsh breathing down my neck, I flicked on the light switch.

"Oh my God!" Thor came tearing toward me, winding his way in and around my ankles. "Where have you been? Do you know what time it is? Do you? Huh?"

Walsh laughed. "Someone's happy to see you."

In imminent danger of tripping over the talkative feline, I leaned down and scooped Thor into my arms. "He thinks he's in danger of starving." I replied. "Which isn't the case, but he does like to let me know that his food bowl is getting to dangerously low levels."

"You may mock me," Thor purred as he head bumped my chin, "but it's true."

"Just because you can see the bottom of your bowl doesn't mean you're starving."

"I disagree." Knowing it was useless to argue, and very much aware of Officer Walsh chuckling at our conversation, I quit arguing and scratched behind Thor's ears, which resulted in louder rumbling accompanied by the biscuiting motion of his paws.

"He likes that." Walsh commented, reaching out to stroke a hand down Thor's back.

"You like cats?" I asked, leading the way into the living and kitchen area at the rear of the house.

"Sure. I like most animals." He crossed to the sliding door that led onto the deck and tested it was locked. "I'll just take a quick look around and then I'll get out of your hair."

"Thanks. For the lift and… well… for everything."

"All part of the service." He repeated with a bob of his head as he headed back down the hallway, opening doors and sticking his head inside as he went. Sighing, I lowered Thor to the floor and rearranged the kibble in his bowl into a neat little pile. He pushed my hand out of the way, purring as he ate two whole biscuits before sitting back and licking his lips.

"Really? That's it. You were apparently starving but two biscuits is enough to hold you?" Rather than answer, he walked away with his tail in the air, jumped onto the sofa and turned in a circle three times before settling in for a nap.

I could hear Walsh moving around upstairs, then the thump of his booted feet on the staircase. I met him at the bottom.

"Everything checks out. I'll do a walk around

outside and then I'll be off. Lock up behind me, okay?"

"Will do." I stood in the open doorway, watched as he shone his flashlight around the front garden, beneath bushes and shrubs, before heading down the side of the house. He was thorough, I'd give him that, and I'd much prefer to have him here tonight rather than Mills. Mills probably wouldn't have checked the house or the garden, he'd have left the engine running and driven away before I'd reached the front door, I was sure of it.

Closing the door now, I turned the lock and rested my forehead against the heavy wood, dragging in a deep breath. Then I remembered. The bath! Brightening, I hurried upstairs, rushed through Ben's room, keeping my eyes on the bathroom door and refusing to acknowledge I was in Ben's personal space, trying not to breathe in the scent of him as I practically sprinted past his bed.

I paused on the threshold. I'd never been in Ben's bathroom before, never had a need to, and I have to admit, it was quite lovely. Masculine, but not overly so. One wall was dark gray tiles in a subtle hexagon pattern, the remaining three walls were the same tile in white. There was a double vanity with two big circular mirrors above each basin, directly opposite the vanity unit was the bath, tucked in between the wall and vanity was the toilet and at the far end a massive shower. I mean, this thing was huge. Six people could fit in it. The shower head was the size of a Frisbee, and I was torn. Bath or shower? Because the shower looked incredibly inviting.

In the end I settled on the bath. Flipping on the taps, I stripped, tossing my yoga pants and T-shirt into the corner and rummaged in the vanity unit for bath products. I couldn't believe my luck when I pulled out a barely used bottle of Kai Bathing Bubbles. Squirting a liberal portion into the bath, I watched as bubble nirvana ensued.

Steam curled through the air, along with the scent of gardenias. I eyed the bottle before putting it back in the vanity—it had to belong to one of Ben's ex-girlfriends because I really couldn't see him soaking in a gardenia-scented bubble bath. But he wasn't around to ask, he was out searching for runaway ghost Myra Hansen, which meant I had some much needed alone time.

Eying myself critically in one of the round mirrors, I peered at my bruised shoulder and what I could see of my hips. Bruised and battered for sure, but still standing. Kinda my motto. What I wasn't impressed with were the dark shadows under my eyes. Rubbing my hand on the mirror to wipe away the steam, I peered closely. Yep. A red hot mess Fitz.

"I really need to buy some concealer." I said to my reflection. She nodded in agreement. Turning my attention back to the bath I was surprised to find it half full already, although the big waterfall spout probably had something to do with the rapid filling ability. I was kicking myself that all the time Ben had lived in this house, I'd had no idea he had such a luxurious bathroom upstairs. Lifting one leg over the side, I carefully eased myself in, sighing in bliss as the warm water surged around me as I lowered my ass into the bubbly goodness.

Leaning back, I left the tap running while I stared up at the ceiling. *Do not fall asleep, do not fall asleep,* I chanted in my head. Especially with the tap running. The last thing I needed was to flood the bathroom. While the bath continued to fill around me, I thought about Myra's case. I was convinced her murder was connected to the bank robbery. And I was convinced her boyfriend, Lee, was involved in the robbery. But what I had was no evidence, only my gut instinct, and despite having the ability to talk to ghosts, Myra hadn't coughed up anything useful and was now MIA.

My mind drifted back to my break in. Had it

been Lee or one of his men? A memory flashed behind my eyes, of the figure, dressed all in black, hurrying away as I dangled from the railing. He hadn't been overly tall. And he'd had a belly. Not the tall, slim builds of the men involved in the holdup. I frowned, squeezing the top of my nose between my thumb and forefinger. The intruder's clothes had looked oddly bulky, like he'd pulled them on over his day clothes.

I shot up in the bath, water sloshing. "Mills!" Flicking off the tap, I clapped my hands to my cheeks. What if my intruder had been Officer Mills? Oh my God, it all made sense. He'd been hounding me all day, clearly had some beef with me—although I was at a total loss as to what I'd done to warrant such attention. But the intruder had been of similar height and similar build, right down to the gut hanging over his belt. And when I'd called it in, he'd gotten there pretty fast, which again made perfect sense if he was the guilty party. All he had to do was return to his car, strip out of the black sweatpants and hoodie, then pretend he'd just arrived. He'd made sure to touch my stuff without gloves, so if any prints or DNA turned up, he had a reasonable explanation.

"What a weasel." I reluctantly abandoned my

bath, wrapped myself in the robe hanging on the back of the door and headed downstairs for my phone. I had to call Galloway and tell him my suspicions about Mills. I was at the foot of the stairs when I heard a jiggling at the front door. Officer Walsh must be testing I'd actually locked up behind him. Crossing to the door, I flung it open. "Oh good, I'm glad you're still here, I just remembered something…" I trailed off in horror when I saw who was standing on my doorstep.

20

Clutching the lapels of the bathrobe, I eyed Lee Noble up and down. Dressed in dark jeans and the same black leather jacket I'd seen him in earlier, he blended in perfectly with the night.

"Oh sorry. I thought you were someone else." I shuffled slightly to put the door between us.

"Yeah? Who? That cop? Nah, he's long gone." Lee pushed the door, hard, and I staggered back as he forced his way inside. I closed my eyes on a prayer. Galloway was going to be so pissed at me. Not only didn't I turn on the alarm—in my defense I was waiting for Ben to return to instruct me on how to do it—but I'd also just opened my door without knowing who was on the other side. I was going to lose PI points over this, I just knew it.

"Oh, by all means, come on in." I snapped, swinging the door shut and following him. "What can I do for you, Lee?"

"Drop the case." He stood next to the dining table, hands on hips, and looked around. "Nice place." He added.

"Drop the case?" I repeated. "You don't want me to find out who killed Myra? Your girlfriend."

"You're sticking your nose into business that doesn't concern you. And you know what happens to little girls who stick their noses in?" He cracked his knuckles and took a menacing step toward me. His intimidation game was strong, and I was sorely tempted to take a step back, but then I'd be playing his game, buying into his tactics, and that simply wasn't how I rolled.

"They solve the crime!" I grinned. He paused, taken aback, then his face darkened. Thor, who until now had been asleep on the sofa, lifted his head. "Cor, this one's been watching too much Thug Life." He stretched, then sat. "Are we in trouble here?"

I turned my head slightly, giving Thor an imperceptible nod. I almost sagged in relief when the hackles along his back stood on end. "Right you are." His British accent thickened with stress it seems. "You need me to call someone? Like last time?"

"Good idea." I said out the corner of my mouth.

"What's that?" Lee cupped a hand around his ear. "You say something? Because let me tell you little lady, the words coming out of your mouth right now ain't music to my ears."

Like I cared. Sexist pig. All his good *little girl* and *little lady* comments grated on my nerves, not to mention using the sheer physical size of a male compared to a female as intimidation. The old, do what I tell you to do or I'll hurt you. I wondered then if Myra had been a victim of domestic abuse. I didn't have time to ponder it for long though, seems Lee got tired of me not playing his game. He stormed toward me, and I knew he expected me to cower or run. Instead, I held my ground.

Was I scared of him? Of course I was, I wasn't an idiot. But I also knew how to defend myself and the last time a man had raised his fist to me I'd left him curled up on the floor nursing bruised balls. Crude but effective. Thor jumped off the sofa and disappeared.

"Smart cat." Lee sneered, "at least one of you has some brains." Then he launched at me. I ducked, avoiding the fist gunning for my face, then hooked one foot behind his ankle, planted my weight and swung around, sweeping my other foot out wide as I put myself behind him.

"What the?" He swung around, searching for me, only I was ready for him, right up in his face, or more importantly, my knee was right up in his business. The crunching noise took us both by surprise. I froze, knee in his groin, eyes on his face, while his own eyes widened then went cross-eyed. He made a strange noise but other than that, didn't move. I wasn't even sure he was breathing.

I could hear Thor talking in the background, meowing to God only knows who, but ever since he'd learned the trick of operating my phone, he'd taken to calling people randomly. Usually he managed to pull up my last call and simply hit re-dial with his paw. But the trick Ben had taught him had saved my hide, so I had zero complaints that my cat was running up my data plan.

Standing on one foot was not a skill I could sustain for any amount of time, so I removed my knee from Lee's nether regions and stepped back, far enough that I was out of punching distance, but close enough I could jump in and give him another taste of Fitzgerald medicine if he made any sudden moves.

He didn't. He toppled and there was nothing graceful about it. Over he went, sideways, hitting the floor with a crash, his skull bouncing so hard I flinched. Thor was still chatting away, and I spared him a glance. He'd pulled my phone out of my bag that I'd tossed onto the dresser in the hallway and was now sitting next to it, giving whoever was on the other end a blow by blow account of what was happening. At least that was what I assumed, but as I skirted around Lee and got closer, I heard what Thor was actually saying.

"I mean," he flicked his tail, "I don't think it's too much to ask to keep my bowl fully stocked, right? But you're right, it probably won't be an issue now she's finally moved in. Living here part time just wasn't working for me, I need round-the-clock care."

"Thor!"

He jumped in surprise, leaped into the air and landed on the floor gracefully. "All taken care of?" He asked, craning his head around to get a look at Lee, who still hadn't moved or uttered a sound. I was starting to feel concerned.

"I thought you were calling for help?" Picking up my phone, I held it to my ear. "Hello?"

"As much as I enjoy my chats with your cat,"

Galloway drawled in my ear, "you probably should lock your screen so he can't use your phone."

Yeah, but then he couldn't call for help when I needed it. Not that he'd been as much help this time around, but still.

"Yeah, yeah." I carried the phone back into the living room to keep an eye on Lee. "You remember that time when a guy came to my house and tried to punch me and I kneed him in the nuts?"

"Yeeeees. Why?"

"It's kinda happened again. Well, not kinda. It has. It has happened again."

A full three second's of silence. "What am I going to do with you?" He sighed.

"Well, not arrest me would be good. But if you could come arrest Lee Noble, that'd be great."

"It's Noble? You should have led with that!" A flurry of activity in the background, Galloway barking out orders. "We've just issued an arrest warrant for him."

"For Myra's murder?"

"For the bank robbery. We found the van."

"Where?"

"In the garage of Eli Duffy." Galloway said. "Eli, it seems, is not the smartest tool in the shed. Noble had told him to hide the van. So he did. In his own garage. Correction. His mom's garage 'cos he still lives at home. When she asked him to take some garbage to the tip, he used the van. A patrol recognized it, and with it not sporting plates, pulled him over."

"Nice." I grinned.

"It gets better."

"Oh?"

"Eli hid his share of the loot in the van. It wasn't much—we already knew that—so he stashed it in the glove box."

I snorted. "Smart."

"Right? Anyway, he's young and stupid and was scared witless when we arrested him. He rolled on Noble straight away, said it was all his idea, he'd arranged the whole thing."

"Well, he's here whenever you're ready." I offered. Lee was starting to stir, rolling to his side and curling into a ball. I cocked my head and watched as he groaned, long and loud, then pushed up onto his hands and knees. "Actually, he's starting to shake it off I think," I told Galloway, "so the sooner the better might be best."

"Patrols already on the way. Go lock yourself in the bathroom."

Holding the phone away from my ear, I looked at

it in shock. *Lock myself in the bathroom? Was he nuts?* It was like he didn't know me at all.

"Pft." I hung up, then pulled up my voice recorder app and hit record.

"Helps on the way." I said to Lee. He lifted his head to shoot me a glare, started to crawl but then stopped on a hiss of pain. I walked around him, into the kitchen, opened the freezer and took out the bag of frozen peas I'd used on my shoulder. I tossed them at him, winced as they smacked him in the side of the head. I couldn't have aimed better if I'd tried.

"Try those." I offered. "Might help."

"Bitch." He ground out, grabbing the peas and shoving them down the front of his pants. Gross. Those peas were going in the bin after this.

"It was you, wasn't it, who shot at me down at the docks?"

"Too bad we missed." He spat. "Would have saved all this trouble now."

"I'm not sorry at all." I grinned, plopping myself on one of the bar stools at the kitchen island and placing my phone on the bench. "For one, I wouldn't have missed this. This," I waved at him on the floor, "is priceless." Then I sobered. "But you made me roll my best friend's car. That wasn't cool."

"I heard you had an *accident*." He sneered.

"Accident my ass. You were chasing me. Shooting at me. Trying to kill me." It was sobering, saying it out loud. I wished Ben were here, for despite all my bravado with Galloway, the reality of having Lee Noble force his way into my house and threaten me was, quite simply, horrifying.

"Was Myra with you?"

"Not at the docks."

"But she was earlier. She was your getaway driver, wasn't she?"

Lee looked at me, not saying a word. "Oh, don't worry, you can tell me. The police were on the way to arrest you, anyway. Some guy called Eli told them the whole thing." I couldn't keep the glee out of my voice.

"That snitch." Lee growled. "He'll pay for this."

"I'm sure he already told the cops who your little gang is. Face it, Lee. You're busted. But tell me something… Ashley Baker. Is she involved in this? After all, you and your pal Rhys setup her sister to take the fall for drug smuggling."

Lee snorted, then with one hand clutching the peas down his pants, he hobble crawled, pulling himself to his feet using the sofa as leverage. I watched him carefully. I'd be ready if he decided to launch himself at me.

"Quite a surprise seeing Ash here." Lee said, breathing deeply. I could see sweat beading on his forehead. Good. Pain was still high, which meant movement would be slow. I was safe. Blow me down with a feather when he pulled a gun from the back of his waistband and aimed it at me.

21

"*S*hit." I whispered. I hadn't counted on a weapon. Hadn't thought to search him for one either. Gonna lose even more PI points. Slowly, I raised both hands.

"You going to shoot me now, Lee?" I asked.

"Pretty much." He agreed.

"Before you do, one thing?"

"What?"

"Myra? I can't go to my grave not knowing…"

He studied me, gun aimed at my heart, considering his options I assumed. I mean, he could pull the trigger and leave my curiosity unsatisfied. But then he could gloat. Be proud of the murder he'd gotten away with. For I was sure he'd killed her, I just couldn't understand why. And I had no proof.

For the longest time I'd thought it was Jacob, that his quirky, obsessive nature had been the impetuous behind Myra's murder.

"Okay sure, why not?"

I blinked. He'd fallen for it. My ploy to buy time. Didn't he believe me when I said the cops were on their way? Maybe he thought he had enough time to gloat, then kill me, then get away? But I'd take this, I'd take his ego over dying.

"So you're saying, just to be clear, that you *did* kill Myra?" Once more for the recording please Lee.

The hand holding the gun waved in the air as he spoke and it was all I could do not to duck. "Yeah, I did it. Silly cow didn't even see it coming."

"Well no, I wouldn't have thought so considering you stabbed her in the back."

He chuckled. He actually chuckled. "Good one."

I frowned. "What?"

"I said, she didn't see it coming. Cos she was a psychic." Oh. He was laughing at his own joke! Pathetic creature he was.

"What I'm not understanding is why? Weren't the two of you in love, getting married?"

"You like that? That was a little seed I planted with young Ash. Despite what happened to her sister, she's so naïve."

"I'm really not following."

"Lemme dumb it down for you." Lee sighed, adjusting the frozen peas. I refused to lower my eyes to his crotch, instead kept them glued to his face. "Myra and I are two of a kind."

"Thieves? Frauds?"

Lee shrugged, "Doesn't matter what label you give us. We were the same, me and her. Always thinking, always scheming. Only I was one step ahead of her."

"How?" I asked.

"She thought we were in it together." He shrugged.

The penny dropped. "Ohhhhh. You were intending to rip her off? Take her share of the spoils? Or trick her into giving it to you. Was the plan always to kill her?"

"I know she can be a vindictive bitch, I wasn't taking any chances with her. We'd do the job, get the cash, leave town."

"Leave town?"

He glanced around, as if checking no-one could overhear us. "The plan was to rob the bank, announce I had a new job in La Tireno and that Myra was moving with me. Only she wouldn't make it to the new destination. No one would miss her.

Everyone we left behind in Firefly Bay would assume she was with me. And no one in La Tireno would have been expecting her. She'd simply disappear."

"But her business? Her clients?"

"I have all her logins and someone lined up to take care of her website. A nice little side earner."

"And she didn't know any of this? That you were planning to cut her out?"

"How would she? She's not a psychic! She's just damn good at reading people's body language. Smart too. Just not smart enough for me."

Oh, the irony. Myra Hansen had been duping and deceiving her clients only to be deceived herself by the one person closest to her. I wonder if she knew when she woke up dead? Did she figure it out, that it was Lee who killed her, and that's why she was so upset? That the player had been played, and she'd had no clue?

"What happened to change your plans then? Why did you kill her in Nether & Void? No way you can write off a knife in the back as an accidental death. No way that was going unnoticed."

"Yeah," He grinned sheepishly, "my temper got the better of me I'm afraid."

"Because of the money?"

"We were meant to get hundreds of thousands. What we got was a pittance. And we'd blown it. No way we could hit the bank again. But Myra had convinced herself that she could work the bank guy angle harder, had a plan to slip a trojan into his laptop, but she needed to get access to it first." He snorted. "I told her the guy wasn't stupid, that with the police asking questions he'd start to put two and two together." Lee Noble was right. Jacob had figured out he'd accidentally leaked classified information to Myra.

"So you got angry... and killed her?"

"We were fighting. In her shop. She said she'd ask the cards what to do, that she'd do a reading, and was sitting at her table shuffling the stupid things like it was real!" His voice went up. "There was a knife she used for cutting up fruit. It was laying there. I picked it up and stabbed her."

Then he leveled his gaze on me, along with the gun. "And now it's your turn."

I held out my hands. "Wait?"

"What now," He sighed, "because I really need to get outta here and you're just slowing me down."

"For this!" Thor ran up the back of Lee's body and attached himself to Lee's bald head, all four paws gripped tight, claws embedded.

"Argh!" Lee tried to pry Thor off with one hand, staggering and crashing around, the hand with the gun waving wildly. I lunged for it, sending up a silent prayer it wouldn't go off and accidentally shoot me, because that would really suck.

"Hold on, Thor." I grunted, two hands gripping Lee's wrist and trying to pry the gun from his grip.

"Oh, I am. Watch this!" Thor sounded like he was having way too much fun. As the three of us staggered around the living room, Thor scratched and clawed, maneuvering himself so his butt was in Lee's face.

"Classy." I puffed, finally wrenching the gun free.

"Police! Freeze!"

I shuffled backward, out of Lee's reach, and held up my hands, the gun aloft in my left hand. Officer Walsh, gun drawn and aimed at Lee who was still trying to dislodge Thor, glanced at me. "You okay?"

"Yes." I nodded. "I'm just going to put this down, okay?" I jerked my head at the gun in my hand. I was making myself nervous holding it. What if I accidentally shot someone, myself included?

Officer Walsh skirted around Lee, not taking his eyes off him, "I'll take it." As he eased the gun out of my hand Thor suddenly howled in pain.

"Don't you hurt my cat!" I screamed, launching

myself at Lee who had punched Thor in the side. Oh, my poor kitty. I was raising my knee for another jab to his jewels when Galloway's shout startled us all.

"For the love of God, FREEZE!"

We did. Even Thor. Slowly, I lowered my leg before I fell over. "Can I get my cat?" I whispered.

"Can she please get her cat!" Lee echoed.

"Affirmative." Galloway said, appearing in my line of sight, gun drawn.

"Thor? Good boy, but you can come down now. Come here." I coaxed.

"You're sure? Cos I'm happy to stay here and scratch him up some more. There are some spots not bleeding."

"Gracious offer, but no, we're done. Come here, I'll catch you." Thor retracted his claws and leaped into my waiting arms. I cuddled him close, running a hand over his fur. "You okay? Are you hurt?"

Thor snuggled in under my chin. "He winded me, that's all. Who hits a cat? Asshole."

Lee, who was standing with both hands in the air, a pack of frozen peas shoved down his pants, and a bald head that was now scratched up and bleeding profusely, looked at us in utter astonishment. "Are they... talking to each other?"

Officer Walsh whipped out his handcuffs,

securing Lee's hands behind his back. "Lee Noble, you're under the arrest for armed robbery."

"And murder." I interjected. I grabbed my phone off the counter and stopped the recording. "I have it all here. He admitted to killing Myra."

"You recorded it! You bitch!" Lee twisted and turned in Officer Walsh's grasp, trying to lunge for me.

Galloway holstered his gun. "Get him out of here."

"Yes, Sir!" Officer Walsh jerked Lee, pushing him toward the front door.

"Easy, man." Lee groaned. "She's ruptured a bloody ball. I can barely stand, let alone walk."

"Oh yeah, he may need medical attention." I called after them.

Galloway turned to me, mouth open as if to speak, then slowly closed it and just looked at me.

"What?" Oh good grief, don't tell me I had pizza sauce down my shirt? I mean, it wouldn't surprise me, but I'd been extra vigilant while eating pizza earlier this evening. I checked. Nope, no sauce stain. Because I wasn't wearing a shirt. I'd belatedly forgotten I was wearing nothing but a bathrobe. Galloway's eyes darkened to a stormy gray as he looked me up and down before his eyes came back to mine. The heat in them was unmistakable.

An answering spark curled through me, heating me from top to bottom, curling into my abdomen. I could feel the flush of it in my cheeks. Galloway could too, for he lifted one hand and slid his palm over my cheek, cupping my face. I instinctively nestled further into his touch. That spark soon turned into a flame and I was pretty sure I was melting, for now my legs were incapable of holding my weight.

Seeing me wobble, Galloway slid his hands beneath my arms and lifted me onto the kitchen island, leaning into me. My legs locked around the back of his thighs of their own volition—*I swear they have a mind of their own!*

With our faces inches apart, his breath hot on my lips, he looked deeply into my eyes. So deep I swooned, and I'm not a swooner, but by hell, Captain Cowboy Hot Pants had some real serious seductive juju going on.

"The first time I kissed you, you kinda freaked out. The second time I kissed you, we were interrupted." He said in a voice that made my knees weak.

"Third times the charm." I replied, my voice all breathy and unfamiliar to my own ears.

"And I promised you I could wait."

I nodded. "That you did." I remembered, after our first kiss.

"And the next move would be up to you. When you were ready."

"Right." I breathed. Why was he even talking? Why wasn't he kissing me? We'd gotten past my freak out, hadn't we?

"I need you to be sure, Audrey. One hundred percent. Because they'll be no stopping this time." He growled. I was more than ready. I was beyond ready. I was so ready I was more than prepared to rip his clothes off and have my way with him here on the counter. And then through my passion addled mind the penny dropped. He was waiting for me to make the first move, for me to kiss him. No problem, Captain Cowboy Hot Pants, brace yourself, I'm coming in.

Sliding my arms around his neck, I pressed my lips to his, swept my tongue along his lower lip and kissed him like my life depended on it. All of my soft melded against all of his hard and everything south of my bellybutton clenched in anticipation. I was practically purring when his tongue met mine and his hands expertly discovered my body. I breathed out a moan when his hand cupped my breast through the bathrobe and his mouth grazed across my cheek to my ear, nipping it with his teeth.

I returned the favor and tried to memorize every muscle, every hard ridge, but his clothes were in the way. *Too many clothes!* Sliding my hands across his shoulders, I grabbed fistfuls of his sexy as sin lumberjack slash cowboy checkered shirt and pushed it off his shoulders and down his arms. He removed his hands from my body long enough to untangle himself from the shirt while I set to work on the T-shirt beneath, tugging the hem up toward his head, revealing the rock-hard abs I'd been dying to taste. I couldn't help myself. I licked him. He growled. I melted.

22

"What are you doing? You can't do this to me!" A woman's voice screeched, and I jerked then froze, my brain trying to comprehend what my ears were hearing. There was a woman here? Did Galloway have a girlfriend? Had she followed him here? How did she get in the house? The Police had left and closed the door behind them, I remember hearing it.

"I can and I will." Ben yelled and I almost sagged in relief. It was just Ben. Then I froze again. Who was the woman? Did he find Myra? Was she with him now?

"Listen, you two bit private detective wanna be—"

"Wanna be?" Ben cut her off. "Lady, and I use that

term loosely, I was a detective with the Firefly Bay Police Department before I was a PI. No *wanna be* about it."

"Oh yeah? Well, look at you now, hotshot. Dead as a doornail." Although I couldn't see her, I could imagine the sneer on her face.

"Right back at ya." Ben drawled. "Fool me once, shame on you. Fool me twice? Oh no, I'm on to you, Myra Hansen. If that's even your real name."

She sniffed and didn't answer. I took that as my cue to find out what the hell was going on. *Why was Myra in my house?* I pushed against Galloway's chest and eased down from the countertop, tightening my loosened robe as I padded down the hallway to the front foyer where two angry ghosts were glaring at each other.

"What's going on?" I asked Ben. Myra turned and eyed me up and down, a distasteful expression on her face. "Oh here she is, your little pet detective."

"Hey, I'm no-one's pet!" I protested. Boy, had she had an attitude adjustment since we found her howling in her store. I narrowed my eyes, studying the ghostly visage before me. Unlike Ben, who was a washed out version of his human self, Myra had taken on an orange hue. I cocked my head, wondering if it was her aura gone haywire. *Did ghosts even have auras?*

"Myra's a fake!" Ben pointed an accusatory finger at Myra, who slapped it down. Only they couldn't touch, instead where their limbs connected shattered into a weird ghostly snow storm type effect. Shaking my head, I focused on what Ben had said. "Yeah, I know. I was here when Galloway told us. But, quick question," I planted my hands on my hips and cocked my head at Myra. "What's she doing here? How did you get her here? And why?"

"That's three questions." Ben held up three fingers in what I guessed was meant to be a rude gesture.

"Whatever. Now spill."

"She tricked me earlier when I went to visit her at her store. Actually back up. It was before then. She tricked me when she said she couldn't leave her shop."

"Why would she do that?" I asked.

"Because she didn't want me ghosting her every step."

Myra snorted. "You got that right. I don't hang with cops."

"I bet." I muttered under my breath, then glanced at Ben, indicating he should continue.

"So yeah, when I went back to visit her I admit it threw me that she wasn't there. I'd thought maybe she'd crossed over. Which is exactly what she wanted me to think."

I shot a glance at Myra, who shrugged. She was floating several inches off the floor, as if she hadn't quite got the hang of how to control her ghostly body.

I shifted my attention back to Ben. "Actually something happened here tonight that sheds a lot of light on what happened to Myra. A lot of light. A darn spotlight even." I began, and then it happened. That horrible, *horrible*, realization of what I'd just done. "Oh, shit." I whispered, slapping a hand over my mouth.

"What?" Ben asked, probably thinking I'd discovered some pivotal clue. I looked over my shoulder, and sure enough, there stood Galloway in the hallway. Watching me. He'd pulled on his T-shirt, which was a crying shame, but what was worse was I'd just walked out on him mid grope and now I was having a conversation with two ghosts he couldn't see.

Ben followed my line of sight. "Uh oh."

"Exactly." No point in covering now. Galloway

had witnessed the whole exchange. Instead, I turned and smiled. "Coffee?" I asked.

"Are you talking to me?" Galloway drawled.

"I am." I nodded, hurrying past him. In the kitchen I grabbed a pod for my Keurig. There was not enough caffeine in the world for dealing with two fighting ghosts and explaining to my non-ghost boyfriend that I could talk to ghosts. *Wait? I was thinking of Galloway in terms of boyfriend material?* I wasn't sure what to make of that, but right now it was the least of my problems.

Grabbing two cups from the overhead cupboard, I positioned one to catch the liquid nirvana soon to be coming my way. I heard his footsteps as he approached, caught sight of him out the corner of my eye sliding onto a stool at the bench. "You probably think I'm insane," I sighed.

"Nope." I shot him a look. He didn't look mad, which would have been understandable since, from his perspective, I'd suddenly walked out on our making out session and started talking to thin air. He looked... dammit, he looked like Captain Cowboy Hot Pants, his hair all mussed from my fingers running through it, his T-shirt rumpled where he'd tugged it back on in a hurry. But his face, his face, said it all. Curiosity.

"Just tell him, Fitz." Ben said. "There's no way you can bullshit your way out of this one."

"I know, right?" I scoffed. I was screwed.

"He's going to call the psych ward and have you committed." Myra voiced my worst fears.

"Shut up you." I pointed at her. "I don't need commentary from the peanut gallery."

Thor chose that exact moment to come busting through the cat door, trotting up to me with a dead mouse in his jaws.

"I brought you a housewarming present." He said, dropping the mouse at my feet. I jumped back with a screech. "Jeez, Thor!"

"What?" He sat and lifted his back leg to lick his thigh. "It's a present."

"I don't need a present. Especially a dead animal kinda present." I protested, trying not to look at the little carcass on my kitchen floor.

Thor paused licking and narrowed his big orange eyes. "What is it with you humans and not appreciating the presents I bring?"

"Could you just take it back outside? Please?" I pleaded.

Thor began licking his private parts. "I'm busy. You do it."

"You can't stop licking your nut sack for two seconds?"

He didn't even pause, just kept lick, lick, licking.

"Fitz?" Ben said. "You should probably deal with Kade."

"Shit." I'd done it again. Left him hanging. While I talked with ghosts. And a cat. Running my clammy palms down my thighs, I turned to Galloway.

"I can see ghosts." I blurted.

His lip twitched. "Mmmhmmm."

"And talk to them." I added.

"Uh-huh."

"And they talk to me. And Thor here?" I indicated the big gray cat at my feet who was still licking his balls. "I can understand him too."

"You know," Galloway drawled, "I got that."

"You did?"

"Yup."

"And you're not... freaked out?"

He smirked. An honest to God smirk. It was as sexy as all get out. "You had me puzzled for a while, I admit. And it's probably because I spend way too much time thinking about you than I should, but I figured it was something like that. I assume it's Ben you're talking to?"

I frowned. "You believe me? You don't think it's a figment of my imagination?"

"I believe you." Three simple words. Three simple words that catapulted me into action. I skidded around the island bench and into his arms, planting a hard kiss on his lips.

He kissed me back then, much to my chagrin, held me at arm's length. "Let me take care of that mouse while you bring your *friends* up to speed, huh?"

Maybe I should marry this guy. I mean, who else is not going to think I'm absolutely nuts for talking to ghosts, and who volunteers to take care of the little critters my talking cat brings into the house? I ignored the cold sweat at the mere thought of getting married produced, no matter my ovaries were practically humming with the delight of future little Galloways, I was nowhere near ready for that sort of commitment. Then I laughed. *Getting a little ahead of yourself there, Fitz.*

"He's a keeper." Ben teased, watching while Galloway scooped up the mouse and headed toward the sliding door overlooking the deck. "Go ahead then. Bring us up to speed. What happened here tonight?"

I turned my attention to Myra. "Who do you *think* killed you?" I asked.

"I don't have to answer your questions." She stuck her nose in the air and crossed her arms over her chest. "And there's nothing you can do to make me."

"What are you getting at?" Ben asked, face puzzled.

"I have a feeling Myra knows it was Lee who killed her. That's why you were so distraught, right? Because you were still getting your head around the fact that the man you loved—and trusted—plunged a knife through your heart."

Her reaction wasn't what I'd expected. She came flying across the room so fast I slid off the back of the stool in surprise and landed on the floor with a jarring thump. *Ouch.*

"That's a lie!" She hissed, her face so close to mine I got chills.

"Get away from her!" Ben yelled, grabbing Myra's wrist and trying to haul her away from me. Of course it didn't work and their ghostly particles exploded around me once more. I clambered to my feet, rubbing my stinging derriere. I had to convince Myra to cross over. I had an inkling that once Myra accepted the truth, she'd leave this mortal realm. At least I hoped she would because one ghost was more than enough, thank you very much.

"I can prove it." I said. Myra snatched her arm away from Ben and glared at me. "How?"

I picked up my phone. I'd already forwarded the recording to Galloway, but I still had the original. Hitting play, I watched as Ben and Myra gravitated toward the phone, hovering above it as they listened to the events of the evening unfold.

"Wow." Ben looked from me to Myra and back again. "So it was Lee." Myra was silent, eyes on the phone, but I thought I saw a silver tear run down her cheek and disappear into the ether.

"You knew." I said. She nodded, then lifted her head, eyes awash with tears. "I just didn't want to believe it. I knew he was angry that we didn't get as much money out of the bank job as we'd hoped. But angry enough to kill me? It wasn't my fault the delivery got delayed in traffic." Her chin wobbled, and despite everything, I felt bad for her. A little.

"Why didn't you tell us? When we found you in the store?" Ben asked, hand hovering over her shoulder.

"Because I didn't understand it myself. I didn't understand why he'd done it. I just needed some time."

"Time for what?"

"Follow him. Watch what he got up to. I knew he'd clam up once the police were involved, but if I could just tail him, eventually I'd discover the truth."

"I'm assuming you never did? That what you heard on the recording was news to you?"

She sniffed and straightened her shoulders. "That he'd intended to murder me all along? That was definitely an unwelcome surprise. The rest was true. We'd planned a new life in La Tireno, we were going straight." She snorted. "What a joke. I'd bought every single one of his lies. We were buying an old hotel in La Tireno and renovating it, opening it back up for business. La Tireno is a beautiful island." She sighed wistfully. "Do you think there's really a hotel in La Tireno?" She asked me.

I shrugged. "No idea."

Her smile was weak. "It doesn't matter, anyway. Lee's looking at life in jail. The robbery and now murder. And me? What happens to me?"

"Good question." Even as I said it I noticed a change in her. The orange hue that had been surrounding her had faded. Then a bright light appeared, so bright I raised my arm to shield my eyes.

"What's up?" Ben asked.

"Can't you see the light?" I gestured to the giant orb of white light hovering in my living room.

"Light? I can't see nothing." He said.

"You can see it?" Myra dragged her gaze from the orb to me and back again.

"I can. I think it's for you."

"What do I do?"

"Umm. I'm not sure. Walk into it, I guess?" I had zero experience with white lights and crossing over, but I could have jumped for joy that ghostly Myra was moving on and wouldn't be haunting me for the rest of my days. I glanced at Ben, who was watching Myra with a mystified expression on his face. We hadn't really talked about it, but I wondered now if he wanted to cross over. *And if he did, what was holding him back?*

Then Myra stepped into the light. It flashed even brighter, blinding me, then it was gone. I blinked, trying to clear the spots dancing before my eyes.

"She crossed over." Ben said.

"Looks like." I stood, "Is that something you want? To cross over?"

"What?" He laughed. "No! No way. I'm happy here. I don't want to go anywhere." I almost sagged in relief.

The sliding door opened, and Galloway came

back inside. "Good news." He said. "The mouse was playing possum. I released him in the woods."

"Everything's coming up roses." Ben drawled.

"It sure is." Crossing to Galloway, I wrapped my arms around his waist and held him tight, smiling contentedly when he returned my embrace. "Myra has crossed over." I told him.

"And Ben?" Galloway searched the room, but of course he couldn't see Ben, who waved at him.

"He's still here."

"Hey, Ben." Galloway said, and I smiled. How cute.

"Say Hi to him for me." Ben replied.

"Ben says hi back." I repeated.

"Now what?" Galloway asked.

"Now we tell Ben to get lost while we return to some unfinished business." I reached up and wrapped my arms around his neck, tugging his head down to mine.

Ben made a gagging noise. "I'm going, I'm going! Phil down at number twenty-six is a night owl, I bet he's watching some Rambo movie or something, I'll go visit with him."

"Has he gone?" Galloway whispered against my lips. I twisted my head to check. "Yep. We have the place to ourselves."

"Good." He growled, the stubble along his jaw scratching my skin as he ducked his head and nuzzled my neck. I purred in delight and squeezed his butt. "Don't suppose you brought your handcuffs with you?" I asked.

He froze and lifted his head. "Why, Audrey Fitzgerald! Aren't you full of surprises?" Reaching into his back pocket, he pulled out a pair of cuffs and smiled. Woohoo, I loved playing cops and cowboys!

---

*Are you ready for book three, **The Ghost is Clear**? Get it here:* http://mybook.to/TGIC

Join my newsletter to be kept in the loop: https://janehinchey.com/join-my-newsletter/

Thank you for reading, if you enjoyed **Give up the Ghost**, please consider leaving a review.

If you'd like to find a complete list of my books, including series and reading order, please visit my website at:

https://janehinchey.com

Also, if you'd like to sign up to receive emails with the latest news, exclusive offers and more, you can do that here:

Janehinchey.com/join-my-newsletter

And finally, if social media is your jam, you're

welcome to join my readers group, Little Devils, on Facebook here:

https://www.facebook.com/
groups/JanesLittleDevils/

Thank you so much for taking a chance and reading my book - I do this for you.

xoxo

Jane

FREE BOOK OFFER

Want to get an email alert when the next Ghost Detective Mystery is available?

Sign up for my Reader's Group today,

https://janehinchey.com/newsletter-giveaway-signup/

and as a bonus, receive a FREE e-book of **Cupcakes & Curses!**

Want to read more cozy mysteries with magic and mayhem? Of course you do!

Books in the Witch Way Series:

#1 Witch Way to Murder & Mayhem

#2 Witch Way to Romance & Ruin

#3 Witch Way Down Under

#4 Witch Way to Beauty and the Beach

#5 Witch Way to Death & Destruction

FOR A FULL LIST OF JANE HINCHEY BOOKS VISIT
www.JaneHinchey.com/books

ABOUT JANE

 Aussie Author & International Bestseller Jane Hinchey writes sexy, snarky, badass, urban fantasies and funny, witchy, paranormal cozy mysteries.

Living in the City of Churches (aka Adelaide, South Australia) with her man, two cats, and turtle, she would really prefer to live in a magical town where cooking could be done with a snap of her fingers, and her house would clean itself.

When she's not in her writing cave she's usually playing the Sims, Civilizations or something similar, binge-watching Netflix or upping the ante in the crazy cat lady stakes.

Explore Jane's worlds, get writing tips, and join her newsletter at https://janehinchey.com/join-my-newsletter/ for book news, book sales and laughter! If emails aren't your thing, then join her Facebook Reader Group - Jane's Little Devils!

If you liked this book, please take a few minutes

to leave a review for it. Authors (Jane included) really appreciate this, and it helps draw more readers to books they might like. Thanks!

facebook.com/janehincheyauthor
twitter.com/janehinchey
instagram.com/janehincheyauthor